The Blue
Story Book

Delightful stories for
delightful young people

Published by Granada Publishing Limited
in Dragon Books 1966
Reprinted 1968, 1971, 1974, 1976, 1978

ISBN 0 583 30005 7

First published in Great Britain by
Methuen & Co Ltd 1945
Copyright © Enid Blyton 1945

Granada Publishing Limited
Frogmore, St Albans, Herts AL2 2NF
and
3 Upper James Street, London W1R 4BP
1221 Avenue of the Americas, New York, NY 10020, USA
117 York Street, Sydney, NSW 2000, Australia
100 Skyway Avenue, Toronto, Ontario, Canada M9W 3A6
110 Northpark Centre, 2193 Johannesburg, South Africa
CML Centre, Queen & Wyndham, Auckland 1, New Zealand

Made and printed in Great Britain by
C. Nicholls & Company Ltd
The Philips Park Press, Manchester
Set in Monotype Plantin

Enid Blyton

The Blue
Story Book

Text illustrations by Jenny Chapple

DRAGON
GRANADA PUBLISHING
London Toronto Sydney New York

He ran down the hill

The Sniggle-Snoggle-Snook

The toys in the nursery were as happy as happy could be until the Grumpy Goblin came to live in the pear-tree just by the window. There was a hole in the trunk and the Grumpy Goblin thought he would live there.

But what a nuisance he was to the toys! He popped his ugly head in at the window a dozen times a night and shouted, "Not so much noise there!" just when the clockwork train was having a lovely time whistling and running round the nursery, or the humming-top was practising a nice new hum.

He would come to the nursery fire to warm himself too, on cold nights, and would make the biggest doll sit and read to him for hours. He was a dreadful borrower too – he borrowed the safety-pin that held the bunny's scarf round his neck. He never remembered to give back anything he borrowed, and so you can guess that the toys really didn't like him a bit.

The little clockwork mouse was very frightened of the goblin, because once, when the goblin had been cross with him, he had said he would take away the mouse's key. And then the little mouse wouldn't be able to run about over the floor any more! So whenever the goblin came into the nursery the clockwork mouse hid away.

But the goblin always found him. If the mouse hid in the brick-box the goblin was sure to look there and say, "Ho! Where's your key, clockwork mouse?"

And then the mouse's tail and whiskers would shake and tremble for about half an hour in fright!

If he hid in the doll's house the goblin would be sure to

5

find him there. "Ho! Where's your key, clockwork mouse?" he would say. Once the mouse hid inside the toy motor-bus, and will you believe it the goblin smelt him out there, and the poor little mouse heard his gruff voice saying, "Ho! Where's your key, clockwork mouse?"

The toys were very angry because the poor little mouse was so frightened. They loved the little grey mouse, and never minded winding him up a dozen times a night, so that he might run about and look for crumbs or talk to the little mice who lived behind the wall.

"Can't we stop the goblin from frightening him?" they said to one another. But nobody could think of a way of stopping Grumpy. He only got more and more grumpy if any one scolded him – and if he lost his temper he would chase the toys round the nursery and spank them with a toy brick! What could you do with a person like that?

And then the golliwog had a perfectly splendid idea. Really, it is a puzzle to know how he could have thought of it! It was so good that at first he couldn't tell it to the others – he just stuttered and stammered in excitement.

"I know a l-l-l-l-ove-l-l-l-!" he began. The toys listened. "I've th-th-th-thought of a l-l-l-love-l-l-l-l-!" he went on. Really, he couldn't get the words out quickly enough and he almost choked in his excitement. The clockwork clown patted him on the back and he began again.

"I've thought of a lovely idea!" he said, his words coming with such a rush that they all joined together.

"Iknowwhatwe'lldo!"

Well, what do you suppose his idea was? It really was very good.

"You know that big box of plasticine in the toy cupboard?" said the golliwog, talking quite properly at last. "The funny coloured stuff that Bobby makes flowers and

6

animals from? Well – *I* am good at playing with plasticine, because I tried the other night – and I do believe I could make a perfectly FEARSOME creature with it – and frighten the Grumpy Goblin so much that he won't come near the nursery again!"

"Oooh! What a wonderful idea!" said every one, and even the clockwork mouse squeaked in delight.

That very night the golliwog began to make the fearsome creature. It was Wednesday, and the Grumpy Goblin always went to see his Aunt Gazookaloo that night, so the toys knew he wouldn't pop in. You should have seen the golliwog working away at that plasticine!

First he made a big red body! Then he made a long blue neck and stuck it on to the body. Then he made a great big head and put it on the neck. Then the little mouse ran about and found a match-stick and the golliwog broke it up into bits and made teeth to put in the plasticine creature's mouth. Oh dear, it did look a funny animal!

Then the golliwog made four fat green legs and stuck those on to the red body. And what *do* you think they had for a tail? You would never guess! The teddy bear undid the red silk cord that tied up the nursery curtains, and the golliwog stuck it on to the body for a long, long tail! He made big ears too, and then the biggest doll climbed up on the table and found Nurse's work-basket. She opened the button-box and found two black boot-buttons. The golliwog pushed them into the head of his plasticine creature for eyes!

"It's fine!" said the teddy.

"It's marvellous!" said the mouse.

"It's simply great!" said the clockwork clown, turning three somersaults in delight.

"What shall we call it?" asked the biggest doll.

"It shall be a Sniggle-Snoggle-Snook!" said the golliwog solemnly. He was very proud of himself. Really the

Sniggle-Snoggle-Snook was a very strange creature, likely to frighten any one who met it and didn't know it was just plasticine! The golliwog had another bright idea!

"I'll tie a piece of black cotton to its tail!" he said. "Then we can pull the cotton when the Grumpy Goblin comes, and the cotton will make the tail move about just as if the Sniggle-Snoggle-Snook was waving it crossly. Ooooh!"

So he tied a long piece of cotton to the tail and then, when he pulled the cotton, you should have seen the tail wag! It was most real. The toys shrieked in delight.

The golliwog and the teddy carefully lifted the Sniggle-Snoggle-Snook into an empty box and put it at the back of the toy-cupboard for that night. How the toys longed for the next day to go quickly!

The next night came at last. The toys hopped out of the cupboard and put the Sniggle-Snoggle-Snook just behind the stool where the Grumpy Goblin loved to sit. They worked his tail with the cotton and it wagged beautifully.

"I know something!" shouted the teddy bear. "I will hide behind the coal-scuttle nearby and make a deep growling noise, and the goblin will think it comes from the Sniggle-Snoggle-Snook!"

So he ran behind the coal-scuttle – and then every one went back to the toy-cupboard and waited for that bad-tempered, unkind Grumpy Goblin.

He came along as usual. He jumped in at the window and looked round. Oho! The toys were hiding, were they? He ran to the toy-cupboard.

"Come out!" he said. "Doll, I want to be read to. Golly, I want my hair brushed. Mouse – I want your key! Aha! I'll have it this time! I've lost the key of my clock and yours will just fit it!"

The toys said nothing. The goblin lost his temper and pulled the golliwog's nose for him.

"What's the matter with you all?" he roared.

"Beware of the Sniggle-Snoggle-Snook!" said the golliwog, in a solemn voice. "It's out tonight!"

"Fiddlesticks!" said the Grumpy Goblin. "Never heard of a Sniggle-Snoggle-Snook in my life!"

"Urrrrrrrrrr!" said the teddy bear behind the coalscuttle. It was a lovely deep growl, very like a real Sniggle-Snoggle-Snook might have made. The goblin turned round in surprise. "What's that?" he said.

"It may be the Sniggle-Snoggle-Snook!" said the golliwog.

"Don't believe it!" said the goblin, and he ran towards the coal-scuttle – and then, yes then, he *saw* the Sniggle-Snoggle-Snook! *He* didn't know it was made of plasticine! *He* didn't know that its awful growls were really made by the teddy bear peeping behind the coal-scuttle!

No! He thought everything was real. And just then the golliwog pulled the cotton that was tied to the long silken tail of the peculiar-looking creature – and it moved! Yes, it waggled up and down and shook from side to side too, as the golly worked the cotton!

"Urrrrrrrrrrrrrr*rrr*RRR!" said the teddy bear behind the scuttle.

"Wow!" said the goblin, quite unable to move a step. "Ooooooh!"

"Urrrrr*r*RRRR*rrrr*!" said the teddy bear, and the Sniggle-Snoggle-Snook's tail jerked about like mad!

"It'll eat me! It'll eat me!" cried the frightened goblin, and he tore away as fast as his legs would carry him. He fell over the mat. He fell over a brick. He fell over a book. He fell over himself. He fell out of the window, and he fell down the tree to the very bottom. And all the time the Sniggle-Snoggle-Snook's tail went smack-smack-smack on the floor and the bear said "Urrrrrrr!" as loudly as he could!

9

"That's the last we'll see of the Grumpy Goblin!" said the golliwog. "Oh, how funny the old Sniggle-Snoggle looked! Oh, I really must laugh!"

He laughed – and the teddy laughed – and even the mouse squealed – and the dolls joined in – and even the ball rolled about in glee to think of how the funny old plasticine creature had frightened the Grumpy Goblin.

"He was always frightening us – now we've frightened *him!*" said the golly, wiping, away his tears. "Oh dear – did you see the red tail wagging, everybody?"

They all laughed and talked so much that they had no time to put away the Sniggle-Snoggle-Snook, although the golly had really meant to break him up and put away the bits neatly in the box.

And so Bobby found the Sniggle-Snoggle-Snook the next morning – and how he stared! He never knew who made it, but it was so good that he put it on the nursery mantelpiece and kept it there. It's still there, I know – I saw it yesterday! Good old Sniggle-Snoggle-Snook!

He tore away as fast as his legs could carry him

11

The Tea-Party

Once upon a time there were two children, Susan and John. They were most excited because they were going to a party. How happy they were when the day came at last!

They dressed themselves in their party clothes. Susan put on a frilly dress of white silk. John put on his best knickerbockers and silk blouse with a blue tie. They did look smart.

And then something dreadful happened! The 'phone bell rang – and Mummy answered it. Then she came into the nursery with a long face, and said, "Children, there is no party! Bobby has chicken-pox! Isn't that a pity!"

For a moment Susan looked as if she was going to burst into tears. John went red because he was trying very hard to be brave, and being brave always made him feel as if he was going to burst.

"You will have to take off your things again," said Mummy. "Try not to mind too much. Be brave, and I shall be so proud of you."

She went out of the room. The children looked at one another sadly. What a dreadful disappointment!

"Let's be brave," said John. "It's no use grumbling. It must be much worse for Bobby being ill with chicken-pox on the very day of his party!"

"Let's take off our party things quickly," said Susan. "I don't like to see them on now we're not going. Then let's have a pretend party ourselves, shall we? We can ask all our dolls and toys! It's a pity we haven't got a nice tea-set. There are only a few cups and saucers left, and the teapot got broken last time."

They hurried out of their things. Mummy popped her head in at the door to see how they were getting on. They told her about the tea-party they meant to have themselves, and she smiled.

"Good children!" she said. Then she ran downstairs again. The children put away their clothes, and then got out their little table. They spread a cloth over it and looked for the tea-things. Oh dear! There were hardly any. Even the jug had its handle broken. They set out what they had got, and then chose which of their toys should come to their party.

"Angelina, my big doll, shall come," said Susan. "And Booby, the blue monkey."

"And I'll have Soldier-boy," said John, "and I'm sure Brown Bear would like to come too."

They found stools and cushions, and put the toys up to the table. Then Susan sat down at the head – and just at that moment Mummy came in again, with a big box under her arm.

"I've been to the toy-shop down the road," she smiled, "and I've bought you something because you have been so good and cheerful. Undo the parcel."

They did, in a great hurry – and what do you suppose was inside? Why, a big box full of the loveliest tea-things you can imagine! There was a big teapot with a lid, a big jug, six cups and saucers, a sugar-basin, six little plates, and three big ones! There was a pattern of pink daisies on everything. It did look pretty.

"Mummy!" shouted both the children. "How lovely, oh, how lovely! Just what was badly wanted!"

They set out the tea-things on the table, and they looked beautiful. There was a cup, saucer, and plate for everyone. The Mummy made the children even more excited.

"You shall have a *real* tea-party!" she said ."I will give

13

you some lemonade to pour out, and some sugar-lumps for the sugar-basin. You can have water for the milk and you may get some biscuits from downstairs for cakes. I will cut up an apple for pieces of bread and butter, and you shall have some chocolates for buns!"

Well, what do you think of that? Wasn't it exciting? In a few minutes the little tea-table looked quite different. There was a dish of small round chocolates that Susan said were chocolate buns; a dish of apple slices for bread and butter; a dish of biscuits for cakes; and in the teapot was real lemonade!

Susan poured out first. Every one had a cup of lemonade-tea. Then she poured a little water-milk into each cup too, and put a lump of sugar in. Angelina, Booby, Soldier, and Brown Bear were very pleased to have a full cup in front of them. Then they were each handed a slice of bread and butter. What a fine tea-party it was!

John poured out the second cups of tea. He spilt a little into Angelina's saucer, but she didn't seem to mind. Then they all had a chocolate bun each, and after that, a biscuit-cake.

Mother popped her head in again. "Is there a cup of tea left for me?" she asked.

"Oh yes, Mummy, you can have mine!" said Susan. She quickly washed it under the tap, dried it, and ran back to the table. She poured Mummy out the very last cup of lemonade-tea in the pot. Mummy took a slice of apple bread and butter, and said that really the tea was delicious! She said she was very lucky to be asked to a party, and she did hope every one was enjoying it.

"I love it!" said Susan, and gave Mummy a hug.

"So do I!" said John.

"So do Angelina and Booby!" said Susan, and she pressed them hard so that one said "Ma-ma!" and the other said "Eeee-ee!"

"So do Soldier-Boy and Brown Bear!" said John, and he made the soldier salute, and squeezed the bear so that he said "OOooo-ooo!" in a deep growl. That was his way of saying "Thank you".

"Bobby's mother has sent to say that Bobby will have his party in three weeks' time when he is better," said Mummy. "So that will be nice for you to look forward to."

"Oh, aren't we lucky!" cried Susan. "A tea-party today with a new tea-set – and a real party in three weeks' time! Hurrah!"

"Good things for good children," said Mummy, laughing.

I Don't Believe You!

A little mouse once had a run from its hole in the bank to the backyard of a cottage, where it often found scraps that it feasted on. It listened each night for cats, before it left its hole, and was very careful not to go out if it heard a mew, or saw the ends of whiskers!

Now there was a sharp young kitten at the cottage that knew where the mouse lived and longed to get it.

Its mother taught it how to hunt, and the kitten was longing to show how clever she could be.

"I will catch that little mouse that lives in the hole in the bank, and comes to feast in our backyard, each night!" boasted the kitten. "You will see how easily I can do it, Mother!"

"Catching mice is easier said than done!" said the wise old mother-cat. "They are wary creatures, and need watching and waiting for."

"Ah, but Mother, I have such a good idea," said the kitten eagerly. "There is an old pipe in the yard just near the place where our mistress throws her crumbs, and bits of bacon-rind. The mouse often comes there. I shall squeeze into the pipe, and wait there for the mouse. Then, when it is feasting, I shall put out a paw and catch it! It will not guess I am in the pipe!"

"That is a good idea," said the old mother-cat, washing her face. "But can you get into the pipe, kitten? It is very small."

"Well, I am not very big," said the kitten. "I am sure I can get inside."

"Then I expect you will catch the mouse," said the mother-cat. "Bring it to me when you have caught it, kitten, and I will see how clever you have been."

"Very well, Mother," said the kitten, and ran off to get into the pipe, for it was now dark, and the mouse might come out to look for food at any time.

The little mouse put his nose out of his hole and sniffed the night air. He could smell no enemy smell, and hear no sound except the wind in the trees. So he slipped out and ran through the grass to the back yard where he found so many scraps.

He stood at the hole in the fence and sniffed again. Surely he could smell Cat? He looked all around with his sharp little eyes, but there was no sign of any cat to be seen. He could not hear a sound, so he thought everything was safe. He ran quietly over to the little heap of crumbs in the yard.

The kitten was in the pipe, watching in excitement. As soon as the mouse came near, she stiffened herself — and then, like a flash, she put out her paw and caught the little mouse!

"Eee!" squeaked the mouse in fright. "Let me go!"

The kitten squeezed herself out of the pipe and looked down at the wriggling mouse.

"You are the first mouse I have caught!" she said, pleased. "Aha! I did a clever thing when I squeezed myself into that pipe. You did not guess I was there!"

"Let me go, let me go!" begged the mouse.

Another creature came up, crawling slowly over the yard. It was a fat old toad, whose coppery eyes gleamed in the moonlight.

"What is all this noise about?" he said.

The kitten told him.

17

"I caught this mouse all by myself," she said. "I am only eight weeks old. Don't you think I am clever?"

"Remarkably clever," said the old toad, blinking his eyes. "But how did you manage to catch the mouse? He is a sharp fellow, for I know him well, and have seen him run in and out of this yard a hundred and more nights without being caught. Not even your mother has been able to catch him!"

"Ah, I must be cleverer than my mother then," said the kitten proudly. "But, you see, I thought of a very good idea, toad."

"What was that?" asked the toad.

"Oh, I got inside the pipe and hid myself there," said the kitten. "Wasn't that a good idea?"

"I don't believe you," said the toad solemnly.

"You don't believe me!" cried the kitten angrily. "What do you mean! It is quite true. I *did* get into that pipe!"

"I really do *not* believe you," said the toad. "You could not possibly get into that pipe."

The kitten pushed the trembling mouse over to the toad. "Hold him for me!" she said angrily. "I shall get into the pipe and then you will *have* to believe me!"

She squeezed herself into the pipe. "*Now* will you believe me, you rude old toad?" she said. "Here I am, as you see, in the pipe! Own up that you were quite wrong!"

But there was no reply. The kitten pushed her nose out a bit further and spoke again:

"Do you believe me now, toad?"

Still there was no answer. In a rage the little kitten squeezed herself out of the pipe once more and looked at the place where the toad had been – but he was gone! The mouse had gone too!

"Where are you, where are you?" raged the kit-

18

ten. The mother-cat heard her making a noise, and ran up.

"What's the matter?" she said.

The kitten told her – and the mother-cat laughed till her whiskers shook.

"You may be clever, little kitten," she said, "but the old toad is cleverer still. You will never see that mouse again."

And the kitten never did, not even when she grew to be old and fat. For the mouse had run away to a far hill-side and had made up his mind never to come back again. But before he went he said a few words to his clever old friend, the toad.

"Thanks, old toad," he squeaked gratefully. "Many, many thanks! You did me a good turn tonight! I shall never forget it!"

"Don't mention it!" said the toad and crawled slowly away to his home.

The Poor Stray Dog

There was once a stray dog that nobody owned. He had no name, and no home. He lived in the woods, and found what he could to eat. At night he used to run out and visit the dustbins that stood in the backyards of houses. Sometimes he could push off the lids and find a bone inside.

Often he caught a rat for his dinner, and once he found three pieces of bread thrown away by a tramp. That was a feast indeed for the poor stray dog! But more often than not he went hungry, and he was very thin, so that his ribs showed through his brown coat.

People were not kind to the stray dog. They shouted at him if he came near them. They hit him whenever they could. Then he would put his tail down and run for his life, growling. He thought that people were his enemies, and he longed to bite one of them.

One day he went through the wood, sniffing for food as usual. When he came near to the big pond, from which he drank, he stopped, growling. Some one was there! It was a little boy, sailing a boat. The dog did not like boys. They threw stones at him and they yelled unkind things.

The dog went a little nearer. The boy did not see him. The dog wondered if he could get a good bite at the boy. That would pay back many a blow he had had from the children!

He crept nearer and nearer to the little boy and made up his mind to bite his plump little leg. But suddenly something happened! The boy reached out for his boat – and fell right into the water! The pool was very deep, and the

20

boy could not swim. He shouted and struggled, and the dog watched in surprise.

Why didn't the boy swim? The dog had often swum across the pool, and thought all creatures could do the same. At first he was pleased to see the boy struggling in the water – then a strange feeling came into his heart. He felt as if he *must* jump in and take the little boy out!

So, into the pool he jumped, caught hold of the boy's coat with his big teeth and swam with the child to the bank. He pulled him on to the grass, and then shook himself. A thousand silver drops flew out of his wet coat. He waited for the boy to shake himself too, but the child lay still, panting for breath. Then he sat up and reached out his hand to the dog.

"You kind, good dog!" he said, and tried to stroke him. But the stray dog backed away, growling. He thought the boy meant to get hold of him and hit him. No one had ever spoken kindly to him before, and he ran away through the wood.

When he met his friends, the wild, poaching cat, and the old striped badger, he told them what had happened. They stared at him in surprise.

"How foolish to be kind to one of our enemies!" said the cat, putting out her sharp claws. "What sense is there in that? That boy will only throw stones at you the next time he sees you."

"I know," said the dog, quite puzzled at himself. "But I couldn't help jumping in to save him, somehow. I *was* going to bite him, you know – and then I found myself swimming to the bank with him!"

"You are certainly a foolish creature," said the badger, lumbering off on his big paws. "It doesn't pay to be kind, if you are a wild animal, or a stray one. You should be fierce and cruel."

The dog thought they were right and he was sorry he

had saved the little boy. He ran off alone, and hunted for food. As he came back, late that night, a terrible thing happened to him – he ran straight into a steel trap set there to catch animals in the wood.

Click! The cruel steel teeth closed round his paw, and the dog howled in pain and fright. He dragged at the trap, but he could *not* get his paw away. It was held tightly. The poor stray dog lifted up his brown head and howled dismally. Who had set that trap, he wondered. Maybe that boy he had saved! How he wished he had not saved him from the pool in the wood! The badger was right. It did not pay to be kind.

The dog howled again and again in pain and fright. Far away, in a small cottage, a little boy sat up in bed and listened.

"Oh dear, that's a dog in pain!" he thought. "I wonder if it's caught in one of those cruel traps that have been set in the wood? Just suppose it was that kind stray dog that saved me from the pool, and then ran away! I can't bear it! I must go and see!"

The little boy slipped out of bed, dressed himself quickly, and crept from the cottage. He made his way to the wood and, guided by the dog's howls, came to where the stray dog was held fast by the paw.

The moon shone down and showed him the dog. The boy gave a cry of pity, and went to him at once. The animal bared its teeth and growled, but the boy took no notice. Quickly he pressed back the spring of the trap and the dog took out his paw. He was about to limp off when the boy called him.

"Come here! You must come home with me and let me bathe your paw, or it will go bad and you may lose it."

The dog paused. The boy went up to him and picked him up in his arms. He was such a skinny creature that he was quite easy to carry. He carried the dog all the way home,

The little boy and the dog in the trap

23

and set him down by the kitchen fire.

The dog didn't know what to think. His paw hurt him, and he wanted to bite some one – but he couldn't bite this boy! So he let himself be put down on a soft rug, and he lay there whilst the boy lighted a candle and got a bowl of warm water. Then, very gently, the dog's paw was bathed, and a cool ointment put on it. Then the boy wrapped up paw in an old handkerchief, and gave the dog some milk to drink, and a big biscuit to eat.

"Now I'm going to bed," said the boy to the dog. "You can stay here, old chap. You saved me from that deep pool this morning – and I've saved you from a trap tonight! You were kind to me, and I've been able to be kind to you! Isn't that fine? It always pays to be kind, you know. That's what my mother says."

The dog lay by the warm fire and thought hard. The boy said it paid to be kind – but the badger said it didn't. Who was right? The boy must be – because he had gone to save a dog in pain. The little stray dog blinked his brown eyes in the firelight and thought lovingly of the boy. No one had ever been kind to him before. It was a lovely feeling.

The next day the boy's mother was astonished to find the stray dog in front of her fire. But when the boy told her what had happened in the night, she was very sorry for the dog. She stroked him gently and said: "Poor dog! Poor dog!"

The dog wagged his tail and looked up at her. Two kind people! What luck for him!

"He is half-starved," said the boy's mother. "Poor creature. He has no collar, so he must be a stray."

"Mother, he saved me from drowning yesterday," said the boy. "He is a brave, kind dog, even though he is only a stray. Do you think I might keep him for my own?"

"Yes, if you like," said his mother. So the boy fetched a collar for the dog, and then gave him a fine breakfast.

After that he bound up the hurt paw again, and gave the dog a good brushing.

"You'll be a fine fellow when you are fatter and cleaner," said the boy. You have the loveliest eyes that ever I saw!"

The dog was very happy. He limped about after the boy, and would not let him out of his sight. He licked his hand whenever he could and wagged his tail hard. He could hardly believe that the boy wanted him to live with him and be his dog.

That afternoon he limped to the woods with the boy, who had to fetch some firewood for his mother. The dog saw his two friends, and the poaching cat and the badger, and went up to them, wagging his tail.

"You have a collar on!" said the badger in disgust. "You belong to our enemies! For shame!"

"You are becoming tame!" said the wild cat, spitting at him. "You are no longer wild like us. Shame on you!"

"I came to tell you something," said the dog, earnestly. "You were wrong when you said it was foolish to be kind. Kindness is a great thing, the greatest thing I know, though I am only a dog. If I had not been kind I should not be as happy as I am now."

"Foolish creature!" said the badger in disgust, and he shuffled off.

"Traitor!" hissed the cat, and sprang lightly away. The dog was sad – but, when he heard the boy whistling to him, he wagged his tail and limped quickly off to join him. Better to live with a kind master, than to dwell in the woods with fierce friends!

He still lives with the boy. His name is Brownie, and one of his paws is bent – the one that was caught in the trap. So, if ever you meet a dog called Brownie, with a crooked paw, you'll know his story, and can give him a pat for luck!

The Gobbly Bird

Once there was a witch called Doodlums. She had a black cat called Long-Tail who used to help her in her spells, and sometimes Doodlums used to give Long-Tails sixpence to buy himself a tin of sardines when he had been especially helpful.

Long-Tail was very fond of sardines. He was quite clever at opening the tin with a tin-opener, and then he would eat the sardines one by one and lick out the tin with his rough, pink tongue.

Now Doodlums was not a very successful witch one year, so Long-Tail had few sixpences, and had to go without the sardines he liked so much. He wondered how he might get some for himself, and go to buy the sardines he loved.

But, try as he would, he couldn't seem to think of any way to earn a sixpence!

Now one day the witch, Doodlums, said to him, "Long-Tail, there is a Gobbly Bird nesting in a hole in the old oak tree. I can sell her eggs for sixpence each if no one steals them. Watch that nest for me, please, and tell me each time you hear the Gobbly Bird cackle. Then I shall know she has laid an egg, and can get it."

So Long-Tail went to watch the hole in the old oak tree. The Gobbly Bird was a small, ugly creature, who gobbled up anything and everything she saw and was very much disliked by every one. Witches and wizards liked to get Gobbly Bird's eggs because they were very useful in spells. So they could easily be sold for sixpence, and whenever one of the unpleasant Gobbly Birds made a nest, most of the eggs were taken immediately.

Nobody knew of this Gobbly Bird in the oak tree but Doodlums and Long-Tail. The big black cat sat nearby and watched all day. At five o'clock the bird cackled, and at once Long-Tail ran to get the witch. She took the egg – it was a strange one, perfectly round, and was spotted with red at one end, and marked with yellow at the other.

"Good," said Doodlums. "Wizard Shanky will give me sixpence for that!"

Well, after Doodlums had gone, Long-Tail began to think. Why shouldn't *he* take an egg, sell it to Shanky for a silver sixpence, and then buy himself a lovely, lovely tin of sardines? Oh, what a splended idea!

But how could he get the egg? That was a puzzle. He couldn't get into the hole, for it was too small. He couldn't reach the nest with a paw, for it was too deep in the tree. Long-Tail sat and thought and thought.

And at last he thought of a grand idea. He would go home and dip his tail into the glue-pot! Then he would frighten the Gobbly Bird out of the tree, let his tail down into the hole, and bring up the egg stuck on his gluey tail! Oh, what a really fine idea!

So off he went and made his tail very sticky with glue. Then back he ran and sat on the tree branch waiting for the Gobbly Bird to cackle again. When it did, Long-Tail made a fearful noise snarling and spitting, and the bird flew out of the tree in fright. At once Long-Tail let down his sticky tail into the hole, wagged it about a bit, and then drew it up again. On the end of it was a queer round egg, half red, half yellow!

Long-Tail took it off his tail and set off for Wizard Shanky's. He sold him the egg for sixpence and then raced to the grocer's, where he bought himself a nice tin of sardines. How he did enjoy himself, to be sure!

This is an easy way of making money!" thought Long-

Tail. "Witch Doodlums won't know. I can have as many sardines as I like."

During that week he let down his sticky tail four times into the nest, and each time he brought up an egg which he sold for sixpence. Witch Doodlums wondered why the Gobbly Bird didn't seem to lay eggs, for, of course, Long-Tail did not tell her of the eggs at all. It was all very strange.

Now Witch Doodlums sniffed about one morning wondering how it was she could smell sardines so strongly, when there was not one in the house. Long-Tail was sitting by the fire, washing himself, and the witch looked at him suspiciously. Then she nodded her head, pursed up her lips, and went out of the house, calling to Long-Tail, "See to the house for a few minutes, Long-Tail."

So Long-Tail snoozed by the fire, very pleased and satisfied, for he had twelve sardines inside him. But what was Witch Doodlums doing? Aha!

She went to the hen-house, and collected a great handful of feathers, brown, white, and black. Then off she went to the Gobbly Bird's tree. She popped her hand down, shook the Gobbly off her nest, and filled it up with feathers. The she went back and told Long-Tail to go and watch the nest again. So off went Long-Tail and waited patiently until the Gobbly Bird gave a cackle. He frightened her away, and let down his sticky tail as usual. It came up with the egg stuck on it, but oh! tails and whiskers, whatever was all this stuck on it too?

Feathers! Feathers by the score, feathers by the hundred, black, white, and brown! Long-Tail tried to shake them off, but they were stuck tightly. He shook off the egg though, by mistake, and that fell to the ground and smashed.

He ran down the tree, and raced home, very much frightened to see such a large, featherly tail coming after him. When Doodlums saw him coming in at the kitchen door, she was going to pounce on him and scold him, for by now she knew what he had been doing – but when she saw how successful her feather trick had been she began to laugh.

"Ho, ho! He, he! Look at your tail! Who ever saw a cat with a feather-tail before? Ho, ho, ho!"

Poor Long-Tail! He was so scared – but the worst of his troubles were to come – for as soon as he ran outside, all the other cats were after him in a trice. They thought his tail was a bird! So poor Long-Tail was pounced on time after time, and his tail was scratched and torn with sharp claws.

Those feathers stayed on his tail for a long, long time. Witch Doodlums said she couldn't take them off without pulling his fur off too, so he had to wait until one by one they dropped off, or were pulled off by other cats.

"I shan't steal again!" said Long-Tail to himself. "How was I to know that silly Gobbly Bird would go and fill her nest full of feathers like that!"

It was a long time before Long-Tail got a sixpence from Witch Doodlums again. With it he bought some turpentine to clean his tail – not sardines to eat. Poor old Long-Tail. He won't deceive Doodlums again in a hurry!

The Little Old Toy-maker

There was once a little old man who lived with his wife in a tiny cottage. He was called Stubby the toy-maker, and he could make the loveliest toys. He liked making tiny toys the best – small chairs and tables for dolls' houses, little beds for tiny dolls to sleep in, and things like that. He was very clever at mending broken dolls too. Whenever a doll's face was broken, or an arm or leg, it was brought to Stubby and he mended it lovingly.

Then came a sad time for the old toymaker. Nobody seemed to want his toys any more! All the children had unbreakable dolls which never needed mending. People said his shop was old-fashioned, and they went to the big new store in the nearest town. Stubby went on making his little chairs and tables, but nobody bought them.

"Stubby dear, I don't know what we shall do," said his little, old wife. "We have no money now, you know. You have not sold anything for two weeks. I cannot buy flour to make bread if I have no money."

"Dear me, wife, this will never do!" said Stubby, taking off his big round glasses and polishing them furiously. He always did that when he wanted to think hard, and he was thinking very hard indeed now.

"Have you thought of an idea, Stubby?" asked his wife at last. Stubby nodded.

"Yes," he said, "but it isn't a very good one. You know, wife, our shop window is very old and the glass is not good. Perhaps people cannot see my nice little toys very well through it. Suppose we set out some little chairs and tables and beds on the broad top of the old wall outside?

30

Then everyone would see them!"

"That is a very good idea," said his wife. "I am quite sure that if people saw them, they would buy them. You really do make them so beautifully, Stubby dear."

So out went the old toy-maker and placed six little red chairs and a table to match on the top of the low stone wall outside. Then he put two small beds there as well, and his wife arranged the tiny sheets, blankets, and pillows on each. They did look so sweet! The sun shone down on them, and old Stubby felt quite certain that any one passing by would come in and buy them at once!

But nobody did. Nobody even seemed to notice them. It was most disappointing.

"I'll go and fetch them in after we've had supper," said Stubby. So the two sat down and had a poor supper of one cooked turnip out of the garden, and a crust of stale bread. It was nearly dark when they had finished. Stubby got up and went out into the little garden to fetch in his dolls' furniture.

He walked to the wall and looked down for it in the twilight. To his great astonishment there was none there! It had gone! He felt all along the wall in dismay, and then hurried back to his wife.

"Wife, wife!" he called. "All my chairs and tables and beds are gone!"

"Has some one stolen them?" said his wife, almost in tears. "Oh, what a shameful thing to steal from a poor old couple like ourselves!"

"Never mind," said Stubby. "It shows some one noticed them anyhow. I'll put some more out tomorrow and I'll keep my eye on them!"

So the next day he put out a set of green chairs and a table to match, and one tiny bed. He sat at his window and watched to see that no one took them. But nobody seemed to notice them at all.

And then a strange thing happened. Stubby could hardly believe his eyes! He saw the chairs and tables and bed walking off by themselves! Yes, really — they just slid down the wall and made off out of the gate!

Stubby ran after them. "Hi! Hi!" he called. "What do you think you're doing?"

He made a grab at a chair — and to his enormous surprise, he got hold of a little wriggling figure that he couldn't see!

"Let me go, let me go!" screamed the little creature he couldn't see.

"Show yourself then," commanded Stubby, shaking with excitement. At once the little struggling creature showed himself and became visible. It was a very small pixie!

"Bless us all," said Stubby, his eyes nearly dropping out with amazement. "It's the first time I've ever seen a fairy! Pray what are you doing, stealing my chairs?"

"Oh, are they yours?" said the pixie, in surprise. "Hi, brothers! Stop carrying off this furniture. It belongs to some one!"

At once all the chairs and tables were set down, and many small pixies became visible before Stubby's astonished eyes.

"We are really very sorry," said the first pixie. "You see, we found the chairs, tables, and beds on the wall there, and we didn't know they belonged to any one at all. We thought they were very beautiful, so we took them into the woods to show the Queen."

"Dear, dear me!" said Stubby, flattered and pleased. "Did you really think they were beautiful? And what did the Queen think?"

"Oh, she liked them so much that she said she would like ever so many more," said the pixies. "She has a new country house, you know, and she has been looking every-where for furniture nice enough for it."

"Well!" said Stubby, most excited, "this is really lovely. You might tell the Queen, that I have a great deal more furniture if she would like to see it. I didn't put out my best ones in case it rained."

"Oh, of course we'll tell her," said the pixies. "Good-bye for the present, old man. Take your chairs, and table, and bed – we'll go and tell the Queen all you have said."

Off they went, and Stubby took his toy furniture into the cottage with him, and told his surprised wife all that had happened.

That night there came a knocking at his door – and when Stubby opened it, who do you suppose was there? Yes! – the Queen, all dressed in shining moonlight with a silver star in her hair! She sat on the table and asked Stubby to show her all the furniture he had.

With shaking hands the old man set it out, and the Queen exclaimed in delight. "Oh, what beautiful things you make!" she cried. "Just the right size for the little folk, too. I suppose, old man, you are too busy to make things for us? The humans must be so pleased with your work that you will have no time for fairy folk."

Then old Stubby told the Queen how hard he found it to sell anything, and his wife told her how little they had in the larder.

"We would be so glad if you could buy some of our goods," she said.

"I can do better than that!" cried the beautiful Queen in delight. "Stubby, come and live in Fairyland, will you? Please do! You can make all the furniture for my new country house. And there are no end of little jobs that your clever fingers could do really beautifully. I believe you

33

could even patch up the wings of the pixies when they get torn! "

"Oh yes, I could! " said Stubby, his eyes shining brightly behind his big spectacles. "I'll come whenever you wish, your Majesty! "

So Stubby and his wife left their little cottage one fine morning and went to Fairyland. There the Queen gave them a little white house on a hill, with two pixies for servants Stubby makes beautiful furniture all day long, and he often patches up the torn wings of the pixies.

And once a month he dressed himself up very grandly indeed, and so does his wife. For then the Queen herself comes to tea, and each time there is a new little chair for her to sit in. She is so pleased.

Suddenly lots of tiny pixies appeared

The Jackdaw and the Puppy

Pat was a puppy with a happy tail and a tongue that hung out of his mouth whenever he ran. He wasn't very old, but he was already old enough to go off for little walks by himself and to talk to every one he met.

He belonged to a boy called Tom. Tom loved Pat, and, when he was home from school, the two had fine games together. They both rolled over and over on the floor, the puppy trying his hardest to lick Tom's face, and Tom trying his hardest to push him off. It was great fun.

One day Pat trod on a thorn. It ran into his foot, and he limped home wondering what had happened. He whined whenever he set his foot to the ground. He looked for Tom, but Tom was a school. So the puppy sat down in a corner and waited, holding his hurt foot up in the air. Nobody noticed him.

He stayed there till Tom came home. "Pat, Pat, where are you?" shouted Tom, wondering why there was no little dog to greet him with barks and wags. Pat whined, and Tom saw him sitting in the corner with his paw up.

"Hallo, old chap, what's wrong?" said Tom kindly. He looked at the paw and then turned it up. 'Why, you've got a thorn here!" he said. "Half a minute – I'll soon have it out."

He pulled – and the thorn came out! Then Tom fetched a bowl of warm water and bathed the little sore foot.

"There you are, Pat, that will be all right now," he said, and patted the puppy kindly. Pat was so delighted to have his paw put right – he didn't know *what* to do to show Tom he was grateful. He rolled over on his back with all his paws in the air – he yelped – he licked Tom.

"So you like me to be kind to you, do you?" said Tom. "Well, remember this, Pat – one good turn deserves another – so pass on the bit of kindness I've given you, when you get a chance. See?"

Pat did see. He sat and listened with his ears cocked. Then over he rolled again, and kicked away merrily.

Now a few days after that Pat was running round the field opposite his house when he saw something hopping into the hedge – something small and black. He ran after it in excitement. What could it be? A black rabbit? Oooh! What fun to catch him!

But it wasn't a black rabbit. It was a little black jackdaw with a hurt wing that dragged on the ground. He couldn't fly – and he was very very frightened.

"Hallo!" wuffed Pat, his tail wagging. "I won't hurt you – what's the matter?"

"I fell down from the church tower," said the little jackdaw. "I was in a nest there with my brothers and sisters – and I walked out and tried to fly. I spread my wings all right – but I hurt one of them when I got to the ground. Now I am frightened a cat will get me. I thought *you* were a cat at first!"

"Well I'm not, I'm a puppy," said Pat. "But there's a cat in the house where I live. You'd better be careful!"

"What can I do?" asked the jackdaw, in fright.

"I'll take you to my master!" said Pat. "He'll look after you!" He ran at the astonished bird, opened his mouth and picked him up! How surprised and frightened the jackdaw was! He really thought he was going to be eaten.

He struggled and squawked, but Pat would not let him go. He ran across the lane to the house with the bird, and went to find Tom.

37

And how surprised Tom was when Pat suddenly appeared and put down a little black jackdaw at his feet!

"Whatever's this, Pat?" he said. "Oh, it's a poor baby jackdaw with a hurt wing! Mother! Mother! Look what Pat has found!"

Up came Mother and looked at the jackdaw. "His wing is badly bruised," she said. "Find the old parrot-cage, Tom, and put him in there with a dish of water. Then collect all the caterpillars you can find for his dinner. He will like bread and milk too. If we keep him for a few days he will soon be better."

So they kept the little jackdaw in the cage until his wing was quite better. He grew very tame. He would let Tom pick him up at any time. And when Tom opened the cage door for him to fly away in two weeks' time, he didn't want to go! It was nice, being a tame jackdaw!

But he did fly away, because he badly wanted to tell his father and mother all his adventures. He had a lovely time flying round with his family, though he often went back to talk to Tom and Pat. "You were kind to me, Pat," he said to the little dog. "One day I'll repay you – if I can!"

"Pooh! I don't expect you'll be able to do *me* a good turn!" said Pat. "I'm a dog – and you're only a bird!"

But the day did come, as you will hear. The jackdaw was running about a field with many others, when he heard a motor car coming along the road. Then he heard a loud yelp, which made him jump. The car didn't stop but went straight on – and the yelping went on too!

The jackdaw flew to the top of the hedge and looked down – and in the road he saw poor little Pat, knocked down by a car! Two of his legs were hurt, and he couldn't walk. He was whining miserably.

"Pat! Pat! What's happened!" squawked the jackdaw, hopping down beside the dog.

"That car hit me and didn't stop," said Pat. "Pull

38

hard at my collar and see if you can drag me a bit nearer the ditch so that I will be out of the way of other cars."

The jackdaw tugged, but he could hardly move the dog. So he went to the top of the hedge and called loudly to his companions. "Chack, chack, chack, chack!"

They all swooped to him to see what he wanted. He told them – and in a minute or two there were about twenty strong jackdaws all tugging at the dog's collar to get him to the side of the road.

"Now I'll go and fetch Tom," said the first jackdaw. Off he flew and came to where Tom was digging in his garden.

"Chack, chack!" said the jackdaw loudly.

"Hallo!" said Tom. "So you've come to see me again, have you?"

"Chack, chack!" said the jackdaw, and flew round Tom, pulling at his coat.

Tom was surprised. 'What are you doing that for?" he asked.

"Chack!" said the jackdaw, and did it again.

"I believe you want me to go somewhere with you!" said Tom. He put down his spade and followed the jackdaw, who flew and hopped a little way in front of him out of the gate – down the lane – round the corner – and into the main road.

And then Tom saw Pat! He gave a shout of dismay and ran up to his little dog. "You're hurt!" he said. "Poor old Pat! Never mind – you'll be right now I've found you!"

He picked the puppy up gently and carried him home. Mother rang up the animal doctor, and he very soon came. He said one of Pat's legs was broken, but he would soon be all right again if Tom looked after him well. He *was* astonished when he heard how the jackdaw had fetched Tom!

"The dog helped the jackdaw – and now the jackdaw has helped the dog!" he said. "Well, well – they say one good turn deserves another – but things like this don't often happen!"

Pat got quite well – and once a week he takes a bone to the field and puts it under the hedge. Who for? Guess! Yes – for the jackdaw! Isn't it nice of him! You should hear them talking to one another! It sounds like "Wuff!" "Chack!" "Wuff-wuff!" "Chack-chack!"

They are the very best of friends – and I don't wonder at it, do you?

Oh, Mr. Winkle!

Mister Winkle was always getting into trouble with Mrs. Winkle – and really, I don't wonder at it! If ever there was a silly forgetful, careless man, it was Mister Winkle! You won't believe it but one night he put the dog into his bed, and curled himself up in the baket by the fire. And another day his wife sent him to post some letters, and to buy some new-laid eggs. Well – he got the eggs, and when he passed the pillar-box, he posted those instead of the letters. The postman was dreadfully annoyed.

Now Mister Winkle was ALWAYS losing his fountain-pen. It was most extraordinary how that pen seemed to go.

"I just popped it down on the table," Mister Winkle would say to his wife – "and now it's gone! "

"You mean you thought it was the poker and have stood it up by the fireplace! " Mrs. Winkle would say, crossly – and sure enough, there would be the fountain-pen, standing up straight by the fireplace, and the poker would somehow be on the table.

"Dear me, yes, now I remember," said Mister Winkle. "I wanted to poke the fire, and I did. Then I must have put the pen back by mistake, and popped the poker on the table. Dear me! "

"Well, it's a marvel you didn't put the poker into your waistcoat pocket! " said Mrs. Winkle, impatiently. "Really, you need a nurse to look after you, Winkle."

Now this fountain-pen was always making Mrs. Winkle cross, because it was so often lost and so often turned up in the most surprising places. When it suddenly appeared in a rice pudding, Mrs. Winkle lost her temper.

"Now, Winkle," she said, sternly, "look at that! How did your pen get in the pudding? I suppose you thought it was a grain of rice or something. Well, this is the last time you lose that pen. The very next time you want a pen and can't find yours, I shall go out and find a nurse for you. That *would* be a disgrace! Fancy a grown man like you having a nurse! For shame!"

Mister Winkle was dreadfully alarmed. He couldn't bear the thought of having a nurse. No, no, that would never do. He must really be more careful and try not to forget so much. As for his pen, he must always keep it somewhere safe, where it could never get into rice pudding or by the fireplace.

He went away and thought hard by himself. Then he rubbed his hands gleefully. He would buy a little chain – and put it on the pen – and chain the other end to his waist-coat button-hole. Then, no matter what he did with the pen, it would always have to be with him on the chain!

"If I put it down anywhere and forget it, and walk away, the pen will have to come along," he thought happily.

"The chain will pull it off the table, or off the chair – and I shall never lose it again. Oh, how happy I am!"

So out he went and bought a little chain. When he got home he told his wife all about his splendid idea, and she nodded her head, pleased.

"Where is the little chain?" she asked. "Show me!"

Mister Winkle put his hand into his pocket to get out the parcel with the chain in – and it wasn't there!

"Dear me!" he said, going red. "Where's that parcel now?"

"Perhaps you've posted it, as you did the eggs," said Mrs. Winkle.

"No, I didn't," said Winkle. "Oh, bless me – of course!

I remember now! Look, wife, the shopman put the chain through my waistcoat button-hole so that I shouldn't lose it. There! What do you think of that?"

Mrs. Winkle was pleased. She looked at the little chain, and smiled.

"Now put your fountain-pen on the end," she said, "and you'll be all right."

Mister Winkle felt for his fountain-pen. He usually kept it in his trousers pocket – but it wasn't there.

"Dear me," he said, looking worried again, "now where did I put my pen?"

"Winkle! You don't mean to say you've lost it again already!" cried Mrs. Winkle. "Well, really, I *shall* get that nurse for you – yes, really!"

Winkle looked ready to burst into tears. He hunted round the kitchen. No pen was to be seen. He hunted in the bedroom. No pen there. He stood and thought of all the things he had done that morning. He had gone out to the dog. He had gone to the coal-cellar. He had chopped up some wood. He had read his newspaper. He had wound up the clock. He put his hands into his pockets again just to see if by any chance he had missed his pen, or there might be a hole in one of the pockets.

He felt something unusual there. He pulled it out – it was the key of the clock!

"Oh, Winkle!" said his wife in despair. "How many times have I told you that you *must* put back the key of the clock when you wind it up."

Winkle ran to the clock and opened the door at the back. Standing neatly inside the clock was his fountain-pen, just where the key should be. Quickly Winkle took it out and put the key back. Then he tied the pen tightly to the little chain and put it safely into his waistcoat pocket with a happy sigh. He had got it safely at last – and now it could never, never go away from him.

All that day and the next Mister Winkle was very happy. He didn't forget anything at all. He was as good as gold. You see, he really was trying.

On the Thursday his wife put on her hat in the morning and said she was going out to dinner with her cousin Dame Hoho.

"I've left a nice cold lunch ready for you, Winkle," she said. "All you've got to do is to get it out of the larder and eat it. Now don't do what you did last time – give the dog *your* dinner and eat his plate of biscuits. Just think what you are doing. Oh, and by the way, will you write a note to your brother William, and tell him to be sure and come to tea on Sunday, because I shall be making a fine chocolate cake on Saturday and I know how much he likes a slice."

"Certainly, my dear, certainly," said Mister Winkle, pleased to hear about the chocolate cake. "I'll do that as soon as you are gone."

"Well, make a note of it before you forget," said Mrs. Winkle. "Good-bye!" And off she went.

Winkle thought it was a good idea just to make a note of what his wife had asked him to do – so he took out his pen, and scribbled down on a piece of paper: "Write to William to tell him to come to tea."

He put the piece of paper on the kitchen table and then sat down to read the newspaper.

It was a hot morning – and before Mister Winkle had read more than six lines his eyes closed. Soon there was the sound of loud snoring in the little kitchen – Mister Winkle was fast asleep!

When he woke up it was twelve o'clock. Mister Winkle was surprised.

"Dear me!" he said. "There were such a lot of things I wanted to do! Now I shan't have time to do them. Well – I'll go and get my dinner."

44

He went to the larder and got out a lovely little pie, a salad and a piece of gooseberry tart. He ate the tart first by mistake, and then, thinking he had finished his dinner, he went to wash up all the dishes. He *was* annoyed to find he had put his nice little pie into the washing-up water.

"Now, Mister Winkle," he said to himself solemnly. "This won't do. You know that you said you would turn over a new leaf and not do foolish things again. Pull yourself together!"

He went to the kitchen table and looked at the note he had written there to remind himself of the little job of writing that Mrs. Winkle had asked him to do.

"Aha!" said Mister Winkle. "I'll just write that note straightaway, so I will!"

He put his hand into his trousers pocket to get out his pen – but it wasn't there.

"Dear me," said Mister Winkle. "It isn't there. Now, have I lost it again? I thought I put it in a safe place, so that I should always know where it was. But bless me if I haven't forgotten the safe place. Now was it in the soup tureen? No – it's not there! Was it in the flower-pot? No, not their either. Was it in the coal-scuttle? No, somehow I don't think I'd put it there. Now where, where, where did I put that pen of mine?"

He stood and thought, but it was no use. He could *not* remember about his pen.

"I *must* write that note to William," he said to himself. "But I can't if I don't get my pen. And whatever will Mrs. Winkle say if she comes home, and finds I haven't written to William because I have lost my pen once more? She will certainly go out and find me a nurse, as she said she would – and then I should have to go to bed at six o'clock – oh dear – and wear a feeder, I shouldn't wonder!"

He hunted about a little longer and then gave it up. "I shall get an ordinary pen and a bottle of ink," said Winkle.

"Then I shall write the note with that – and Mrs. Winkle will not know I have lost my pen – and perhaps I shall find it very soon."

But Winkle couldn't find a pen or a bottle of ink anywhere. So he put on his hat and went to ask his next door neighbour, Dame Spink, if she would lend him them.

Dame Spink was shelling peas. She shook her head when Winkle told her what he wanted. "I may have a pen somewhere," she said. "I'll go and hunt. But I know I've no ink. Will you shell these peas for me whilst I go and look?"

So Winkle sat down and shelled all the peas whilst Dame Spink hunted for the pen. She came back with one, but the nib was crossed.

"Here you are," she said. "But you'll have to borrow some ink and another nib."

"Thank you," said Winkle, and off he went up the hill to Mister Middle. Middle was bathing his dog, and he wiped his hands when he heard what Winkle wanted, and nodded his head.

"I think I can let you have a nib," he said. "But you might go on bathing my dog whilst I look. I don't want the water to get cold."

So Winkle rolled up his sleeves and began to bath the dog who didn't like it at all. The dog tried to leap out of the bath, and poor Winkle suddenly found himself covered with white lathery soap. Then the dog shook himself violently and Mister Winkle had a shower-bath of hot water drops! What a mess he was in!

Presently Middle came back with a nib. Winkle thanked him and tried to dry himself. Then he went down the hill to Mother Hoppy's. He felt sure she would have some ink. She was making cakes and was not at all pleased to know that Winkle wanted some ink.

"Just watch and see my cakes don't burn in the oven,"

she said, and went into the bedroom where she kept her ink. Winkle opened the oven door to look at the cakes — but the door was dreadfully hot and burnt his fingers. He gave a yell and danced round the kitchen in pain.

Mother Hoppy came running in with the ink, and when she saw Winkle dancing about and yelling, she dropped the ink in fright, and it spilt all over her clean kitchen floor. Then she saw her open oven door and ran to shut it. Alas! Her cakes were all spoilt! She was very angry and gave Mister Winkle such a slap that he fell in the ink. He rushed out of the house, and didn't stop till he came to his friend's house. Tickles was sitting out in the garden, reading, and he jumped with fright when he saw Winkle rushing in at the gate, howling, covered with ink, soaked with water and holding his right hand as if he were badly hurt.

"What's the matter, what's the matter?" he asked. Winkle told him, and Tickles was very sorry.

"I'll lend you a bottle of ink and I'll take you home," he said. "You look very tired and upset."

He fetched a bottle of ink and then put his hand through Winkle's arm and guided him home. Winkle was very grateful.

He got out his notepaper and envelopes and set them on the kitchen table. He put the bottle of ink nearby, and laid down the pen, into which he had fitted the new nib. He meant to write the letter to his brother William at once, before he did anything foolish again.

"What's that little chain-thing you are wearing on your waistcoat?" suddenly asked Tickles, in interest.

"Oh," said Winkle, proudly, "that's my newest idea, Tickles — so clever, you know! Look, I've got a little chain, and it's fastened to my button-hole. On the other end is tied my fountain-pen, so that I can't possibly lose it. Isn't that clever?"

"Awfully clever," said Tickles. "But Winkle, if you

have your fountain-pen, why do you trouble to go out and borrow a pen from Dame Spink, a nib from Mister Middle, and get burnt and slapped by Mother Hoppy, and run all the way to me to borrow some ink? Isn't your fountain-pen working?"

"Yes, it is," said Winkles. He sat and stared at Tickles, and then he stared at his chained-up fountain-pen. Then he stared at the pen and ink he had taken so much trouble to borrow.

"Oh dear!" he said, in a small voice. "Oh dear! What *shall* I do with myself, Tickles? Here I've chained up my pen to me so that I can't lose it – and I even forget I've got it on the chain! And I've shelled all Dame Spink's peas – and bathed Mister Middle's horrid dog – and burnt myself looking after Mother Hoppy's cakes, and got all over ink – in order to borrow a pen and ink when all the time my own fountain-pen is in my waistcoat pocket! Whatever will Mrs. Winkle say?"

"Don't tell her," said Tickles, comfortingly. "I won't say a word! Now write that note, Winkle, and don't upset yourself any more."

So Winkle wrote the note, and Tickles posted it. Nobody said a word to Mrs. Winkle – but you should have seen her face when she saw Winkle's wet suit and ink-spotted coat!

"WHAT HAVE YOU BEEN DOING?" she said – and poor Winkle didn't know *what* to say!

Harry's Toy Motor-car

Harry had a toy motor-car of his own. It was a very nice one indeed, bright red with blue wheels. There was enough room for him to sit inside it and work the pedals, and a little space beside him big enough for a cat – but not big enough for a person.

Harry went up and down the garden in his car, pedalling away fast. He knew exactly how to steer, and never bumped into the beds of rockery. It was great fun.

But there was one big mistake about his motor-car. It had no hooter. Instead it had a bell! Wasn't that silly?

"I've never seen a real motor-car with a bicycle bell on before, Mummy," Harry said to his mother. "I do think it's a pity. I think it spoils my motor-car!"

"Well, darling, you'll have to make it do," said mummy. "I can't afford to buy you a new hooter. A good one would cost about a shilling."

"That's twelve pennies, isn't it," said Harry. "It *is* a lot of money, Mummy!"

He pedalled off down the garden and into the road. He motored all the way to the toy-shop and looked in the window. There was a hooter there – one shilling. It was a fine one – just right for his motor-car. Oh, if only he could buy it!

But there was no money in his money-box for he had taken it all out to buy Daddy a birthday present. He only got a penny a week on Saturday – and twelve weeks was really too long to save up for a hooter that he wanted now.

He heard some one whistling to him and he saw Tim, the butcher's boy, carrying a basket on his shoulder.

49

And then a perfectly wonderful idea came into Harry's head. Why shouldn't *he* be an errand boy for a little while and earn enough money to buy a hooter? After all, he had a motor-car of his own – he could go shopping for people and could bring the shopping back in his car! What could be easier?

"I'll go and ask Auntie Lou first if she'd like any shopping done," he thought. "I'll see what she says."

So he pedalled down the street to Auntie Lou's house.

"Auntie, do you want any shopping done?" he asked. "I only charge a penny a time, and I bring all the goods back in my car at once. You see, I want to buy a new hooter."

"Dear me!" said Auntie. "Well, I *do* want a few things, Harry, and I'm really too busy to get them myself. Here is the list. Bring them all back, dear."

Off went Harry, pedalling to the shops. He put his motor-car safely outside, and went into the grocer's. He got the tea, the sugar, the butter, and the flour that Auntie Lou wanted and packed them all neatly on the seat beside him. Then into his own seat he hopped and was soon pedalling back to Auntie Lou's. She was very pleased. She gave him a penny and he put it into his purse.

"That's one penny earned!" he said joyfully. "Do you know any one else that wants errands doing quickly and properly, Auntie?"

"Well, there's old Mrs. Brown down the road," said Auntie Lou. "She's got a bad leg. I expect she would be very pleased if you went her errands till her leg's better."

So off went Harry in his motor-car and pedalled up the path to Mrs. Brown's front door. Mrs. Brown was very pleased to see him, and she said, Yes, she would very much like to have him go her errands for a little while, at a penny a day.

So Harry motored off to the dairy to get her the butter

and milk she wanted – and that was another penny in his purse.

On the way home to dinner he met Mr. Donovan, the man who kept the newspaper and magazine shop. He was delivering papers, because his boy was ill.

"Hi, Harry! Could you deliver the papers down your street?" he called. "I'm so busy!"

"Yes, certainly!" said Harry. He packed the bundle in beside him and listened where they were to go.

"Here's twopence for you," said Mr. Donovan. "And you might meet me here tomorrow and do it again for me. My boy will be back on Friday."

"That's fourpence I've earned today!" said Harry to himself in delight. He delivered all the papers, and then got home just in time for his dinner. His mother was pleased to see his bright, happy face.

"I've earned four pennies, Mummy!" he said. "Isn't that good?"

The next morning Harry did Mrs. Brown's shopping again, and that was another penny. He delivered Mr. Donovan's papers and that was two pennies. Auntie Lou had no shopping, but her next-door neighbour asked him to go to old Mrs. White's and see if she could let him have one dozen new-laid eggs.

So off he went and brought them all back safely. He got twopence for that, which pleased him very much indeed. He emptied all his pennies out of his purse that night and counted them – he had nine!

"Only three more and I'll be able to buy that hooter!" he thought joyfully. "Oh, what a good idea of mine it was to use my motor-car for going errands!"

But the next day he wasn't quite so pleased – because Mr. Donovan's boy had come back and there were no papers to be delivered – so he didn't get the twopence. Auntie Lou was away so he couldn't do her shopping.

Mrs. Brown sent him to the butcher's and he brought back some sausages for her. She gave him a penny – so that was one more. And in the afternoon his own mother sent him to buy some cream, and she gave him a penny.

So when he counted out the pennies in his purse that night he had eleven.

"Only one more!" said Harry.

But do you think he could earn one more penny? He just seemed as if he couldn't. Nobody wanted any errands running at all! Not even Mrs. Brown, because her leg was quite better now! It was most disappointing.

"Oh dear, I do hope that hooter won't be sold!" said Harry to himself. "I think I'll just motor along to the shop and have a look to make sure."

So off he pedalled and soon came to the toy-shop. Inside the window was a big ticket, and on it was printed, "SALE NOW ON!"

Harry didn't really know what a sale was. He looked for the hooter – and oh, dear me, it wasn't there! Wasn't that dreadful?

"I shall go in and ask if it's been sold," said Harry, feeling very upset. He trotted into the shop and the shop-woman asked what he wanted.

"Has that hooter been sold?" asked Harry. "I did so want it."

"Oh dear, I don't know," said the shopwoman. "We have got a sale on now, and everything's in such a muddle."

"What is a sale?" asked Harry.

"Oh, we make everything just a bit cheaper for a few days," explained the woman. "Take a penny or two off everything, you know."

"Oh, really!" said Harry, a great idea coming into his head. "Then perhaps that hooter I wanted is cheaper, if only we could find it! May I look round?"

He hunted all round the shop – and do you know, he found it at last, tucked away under a box of soldiers - and instead of being marked one shilling, it was marked "elevenpence!" What do you think of that?

Harry was overjoyed! He felt in his pocket for his purse and took out the eleven pennies he had earned. He counted them out.

"There you are!" he said. "Elevenpence! Now I'll take the hooter. You needn't wrap it up. I've got a motor-car outside for it!"

He fixed it on his car – and off he went home, hooting all the way. You should have heard that hooter! "Parp-parp!" it said. "Parp-parp!"

Wasn't Harry proud – and now, because he has got the hooter he so badly wanted, he goes errands for nothing. Isn't it nice of him! He motors up to Auntie Lou's or Mrs. Brown's and hoots to tell them he's there. He really is a most useful little boy!

The Whistling Pig

Once upon a time there was a very strange pig. His body was made of balloon, and onto it were stuck four legs, a curly tail, and a tiny head. When Jimmy blew him up he looked fine – for he had a great fat body then, and he stood squarely on his four legs like a real little pig.

When Jimmy took out a little cork from the pig's mouth, the air came out of him, and his fat balloon body went down to nothing. As he went small, he whistled – such a sad, piercing whistle, like a very high whine. Then he fell over and lay still.

"He's dead!" said Jimmy. "Now I'll make him alive again!" So he blew him up and stood him on his feet once more, a fat and jolly pig.

He took him to the nursery and stood him on the window-sill. Then he went to get ready for bed, for it was seven o'clock.

The pig stood on the window-sill, and, when the toys came out of the cupboard to play, they talked to him. They did like him – he was such a jolly chap, full of jokes and fun.

He told them stories of the toy-shop he had come from. He told them about a beautiful fairy doll who had sat next to him on the shelf there, and had been sold to go on the top of the biggest Christmas tree in the town. He was soon their very best friend, and even the clockwork mouse, who was a very timid creature, would tell the pig his troubles – how his key was always being lost, and how Jimmy had once stepped on his tail and broken a small piece off.

The toys had one very serious trouble indeed – and that was a horrid little gnome who lived in the garden below, and often came into the nursery to tease and torment them. How they hated him!

"He tore my new sash," said the big doll.

"He pulled off all my whiskers," said the big rabbit, sorrowfully.

"He pulled off one of my wheels," said the engine. "Now I don't run properly."

"He may come to-night," said the golliwog. "He usually does when the moon is full."

And sure enough he came! The pig saw him slip in at the window, a nasty, ugly little creature. When he saw the pig he looked surprised, for he had never seen him before. He gave his tail a sharp pull.

Then down on the floor he jumped and ran to tease the toys. He pulled the clockwork mouse's tail in half. He tore out some of the golliwog's hair – and then he took hold of the poor little baby doll, who was so frightened that she couldn't even cry for help!

The little pig had watched everything. When he saw how scared the baby doll was, he boiled with rage.

He leapt down on the floor and jigged about on his four legs, in front of the gnome.

"Leave the doll alone, leave her alone!" he cried.

"Hallo, funny face!" said the rude gnome. And then, what do you suppose he did? He took hold of the cork in the pig's nose – the one that kept the air in him – and pulled it out!

"I'm dying again, I'm dying again!" cried the pig sorrowfully. "Now I shan't be able to help the baby doll!"

As the air rushed out of his fat body he began to make his loud, whining, whistling noise. How loud it was in the night! All the toys scampered back to the cupboard fright, for they felt sure that some one would hear that

The gnome stared at the pig

noise. The gnome stared at the pig in fear. How could he possibly make such a terrible noise? And what was happening to him? He was getting smaller and smaller – and then at last he fell over, flump, on to the ground, and lay there, quite still.

"I've killed him," said the gnome, frightened.

Just then, the door opened – and in came Jimmy! He had been awakened by the pig's whistling noise, and had come to see what all the excitement was.

He didn't see the little pig, lying flat on the carpet – but he saw the gnome, trying to creep round in the shadows to get out of the window. Jimmy thought he was a rat.

The little boy caught up his walking-stick and hit out at what he thought was the rat. He caught the gnome on his legs, thwack! And again – thwack! Oooh! How that gnome screeched! He leapt out of the window in a trice, and Jimmy stared in surprise as he went – for in the moonlight he certainly didn't look like a rat!

"Well, whoever you are, you won't come back again in a hurry!" said Jimmy, and went to bed.

When he had gone, the toys ran out of the cupboard again, and stood round the poor little flat pig.

"He was so brave," said the golliwog.

"He was so kind," said the baby doll.

"He was the nicest toy in the nursery," said the teddy bear, and began to cry.

"Now he's dead and won't be able to talk to us any more!" said the mouse.

The pig moved himself a little and spoke in a voice like a little breath.

"Don't be silly! I'm not really dead! I'm meant to go flat like this and make a noise! Golly, blow me up!"

How joyful the toys were to hear him speak! The golly put his mouth to the pig's nose and blew. The pig swelled a little. The golly blew again. The pig swelled a little more. Then the teddy had a turn. He had a good deal of breath, so he blew the pig up quite fat. But he wasn't yet fat enough to stand on his legs. So the big doll had a turn and she blew him up well. He stood on his legs and grinned at every one.

"Put my cork in, quick! " he said. I shall begin to make that awful whistling noise again if you don't."

"Here's the cork," said the mouse, who had seen it on the carpet. The golly fixed it carefully into the pig's mouth. There he was, fat and well and jolly again!'

"Did you see Jimmy whack that gnome?" said the pig, pleased. "My, it was a fine sight! He won't come *here* again! "

"It was so clever of you to wake up Jimmy," said all the toys gratefully. "We'll make you king, little pig – and the big doll shall sew you a little golden crown to wear! We do love you so much! "

And now the whistling pig wears a small crown. Jimmy can't think *where* it has come from. Once he took it off the little pig and put it on the clockwork mouse – but the next morning it was back on the pig again!

As for that horrid gnome he hasn't been heard of since!

Down the Rabbit-hole

Jiffy was the smallest pixie you ever saw. He wasn't as big as a baby rabbit. He was servant to six of the ugliest goblins you could imagine – and how he worked for them!

He lit the fires and made the beds, he scrubbed the floor and cooked the dinner, he cleaned the windows and washed the clothes – well, really, there was no end to the things he did for the six goblins.

One day he had a cold. Dear me, it was really a terrible cold! He sneezed and coughed, and he didn't feel at all well.

"Please," he said to the least ugly goblin, "may I stay in bed today? I really don't think I can do any work!"

"What! On marketing day too!" shouted the goblin. "Whoever heard of such a thing! Certainly not!"

So poor Jiffy had to take his basket and go trudging over Bumble-bee Common.

Just as he passed a big rabbit-hole he stopped. He was going to sneeze. He knew he was. It was coming – it was coming – it was – a-tishoo! IT was coming again "A-TISHOO! Oh dear! Oh dear!"

Poor little Jiffy. He sneezed his hat off. He sneezed his ears all crooked. He dropped his basket. He sat down and began to cry because he felt so miserable.

Mrs. Sandy Rabbit heard him. She popped her woffly nose out of the nearby hole and looked all round to see who had been sneezing. She was a big, fat, motherly rabbit and she stared in surprise at Jiffy.

"You ought to be in bed," she said.

"They won't let me," said Jiffy.

"Who won't?" asked Mrs. Sandy Rabbit.

"The goblins I work for," said Jiffy.

"What! Those ugly, double-jointed, snaggle-toothed creatures!" cried Mrs. Sandy Rabbit. "Never you mind about them! You come along down my hole and I'll put you to bed in Fluffy's cot – he's just grown out of it – and you can stay there till you're better."

"But – but – but . . ." began Jiffy.

"There's no time for buts," said Mrs. Sandy Rabbit. "Come along."

She shooed him down her warm dark hole to the bottom. Very far down there was a big room. In it were some beds, tables, and chairs, and a bright little lamp. Mrs. Sandy Rabbit undressed Jiffy, put him on a sleeping-suit of Fluffy's and popped him into bed. Then she made him some hot cocoa.

How warm he was! How comfortable! How delicious the cocoa was! Nobody had ever made him cocoa to drink before. No one had ever tucked him up before – and what was this! Mrs. Sandy Rabbit was tucking a hot-water bottle at his feet. Oh, how perfectly lovely!

Suddenly he sat up in alarm.

"Mrs. Sandy Rabbit! Mrs. Sandy Rabbit! Suppose those goblins come for me?"

"Don't you worry," said Mrs. Sandy Rabbit. "*I'll* tell them a few things!"

Well, of course the goblins were furious when they found out that Jiffy hadn't come home. There was no dinner for them – no tea. The floor was dirty. Their suits were not ironed. Dear, dear, dear!

"We'll go out and look for him, and what a spanking he'll get when we drag him back!" said the goblins. So off they went – and very soon they found his market basket on the ground just outside Mrs. Sandy Rabbit's hole. Oho! So he was down there was he!

Down the hole went the six goblins and came to Mrs. Sandy Rabbit's door. They knocked, "Blimblam, blimblam."

Mrs. Sandy Rabbit opened the door and scowled at them. She pretended that she thought they were the washing come back.

"I hope you've got the clothes clean *this* week!" she grumbled. "Where's the basket? Don't tell me you've forgotten it! And dear me, did it take six of you to bring it this week?"

"We're not the washing," said the goblins.

"Oh, then you must be the men come to mend the clock," said Mrs. Sandy Rabbit. "Which of you mended it last time – because whoever it was lost the key! Just wait till I know which of you it was – I'll pull his nasty little goblin nose for him!"

The goblins began to feel rather afraid of this fierce rabbit. They spoke quite humbly and politely to her.

"We haven't come to mend the clock. We've come to ask you which way to go to find Jiffy, our servant. He seems to have run away."

"And I don't wonder," said Mrs. Sandy Rabbit. "Well, I'll tell you which way to go and what to do – and though I don't say you'll find Jiffy if you do what I tell you, you never know!"

"Oh, we'll do exactly what you tell us, Mrs. Sandy Rabbit," said the goblins eagerly. "Exactly."

"Well, go down the passage to the right over there," said Mrs. Sandy Rabbit, pointing, "and you'll come to a big tree-root. Scrape as hard as you can where you see the root, and you'll come out into a big room of some sort. I don't say you'll find Jiffy there – but you'll find some one all right."

"Thank you," said the goblins and ran off to the right.

They came to the tree-root and started to dig and scrape for all they were worth.

Now, although they didn't know it, a fox and his wife had their den just there, with six young cubs. All the rabbits kept away from that particular passage because they knew that on the other side of the wall of earth lived a family of foxes but the goblins thought that Jiffy was hiding there!

So they scrabbled and scraped and dug for all they were worth. The foxes pricked up their ears and waited. Was this rabbits? If so, what a nice dinner!

Suddenly the goblins broke down the last bit of earth and squeezed through into the fox-hole. The foxes sprang on them – and found them to be goblins and not rabbits!

"Let us go, let us go! " squeeled the goblins, frightened. "Where's Jiffy?"

"I don't know who, where, or what Jiffy is! " said the fox fiercely. "What I want to know is – how dare you make a hole into our den like that! Do you want to be eaten?"

"No," squeaked the goblins, terrified.

"What shall we do with them?" the fox asked his wife.

"Well," she said, looking at the goblins. "There are six goblins – and we have six cubs. That would be a servant for each of them, to brush their coats, take them out for walks, and look after them properly. They can either be beaten – or be our servants – whichever they please."

Well you can easily guess which the goblins chose – and after that they acted as nursemaids to the six spoilt young foxes, who nipped the goblins' ears whenever they were bad-tempered, which was very often!

Jiffy had a lovely time with Mrs. Sandy Rabbit in her cosy little home. His cold soon got better, and he thought he had better go home again – but when he got to the cottage it was empty! There were no goblins there at all!

"Oooh!" said Jiffy, in excitement. "The goblins have gone! I'll get Mrs. Sandy Rabbit to come and live here with all her family – and I'll look after them and be as happy as the day is long!"

So Mrs. Sandy Rabbit and all her fluffy family moved into the goblins' cottage, which was really much more convenient than the dark hole. And there they all lived happily together until the day when the foxes set the goblins free once more.

And, of course, they all came wandering home again to their cottage! Oh dear!

But Mrs. Sandy Rabbit saw them coming up the path. She opened the door, crossed her arms and said, "And now what do you want *this* time? If you're the baker, you're late, and I'll spank the lot of you! If you are the new gardeners, you won't do, so go before I set the dog on you – and if you're nursemaids out of a job, I can tell you of a nice fox-family who have twelve fox-cubs and . . ."

"Ooooooh!" squealed the goblins in fright, and fled away as fast as ever they could. Fox-cubs! Never again! They would go off to the moon rather than look after bad-tempered foxes!

So off to the moon they went. There are no foxes there so they are happy. As for Jiffy, he couldn't be happier. You should see him wheeling out the youngest baby rabbits! They all love him and he loves them – and what could be nicer than that?

The Brownie in a Hurry

Dame Toddle wanted to visit her sister in the village of Long-way-off. There were no buses to take her, and the nearest station was five miles away. So there was nothing for it but to walk!

"I can walk all right," said Dame Toddle, who was an active old lady, "but I hope I don't lose my way. I'll have to keep asking to make sure I'm right."

So she set out, carrying a bag of sandwiches, an umbrella, and a bunch of flowers for a present to her sister.

She walked along and she walked along. It was a warm day and Dame Toddle got very hot. But she trotted bravely on, down the lane and up the hill and over the stile that led through Dimity Wood.

"And now I'll have to ask my way," she said to herself. "For I'm sure I don't know if I ought to go to the right or the left here!"

She sat on a fence and waited for some one to come by. Presently a little boy came along, so she aked him the right way to the village of Long-way-off.

"Go down the hill past the duck-pond and up by the church," said the small boy. "Then ask any pixie you see and he'll tell you which way to go next."

So Dame Toddle trotted off again – and do you know, when she got to the church she discovered that she had left behind on the fence her nice little packet of sandwiches! Oh, she *was* upset!

"Now I'll have nothing to eat!" she groaned. "Oh dear – shall I go back for them? No, I won't. If I do that I'll never get to my sister's in time for tea. I must just go on without them.'

She asked a pixie which way to go next. He pointed across a little bridge over a stream. "Go that way," he said, "and up the hill. When you come to the stop, you'll meet some one called Robin, who knows the way to Long-way-off very well. If you ask him nicely, he'll take you there, for he always goes there about this time of day. Don't miss him now – will you? He's a bit deaf, so you must shout at him and ask him if he'd Robin. Then tell him what I've said."

"Oh, thank you," said Dame Toddle, gratefully, and set off up the hill.

Now there was, not far off, a very naughty brownie called Slick. He was a tramp and very often he stole things. And this morning he had crept along by a cottage and had seen a fine chocolate cake set out to cool on a window-sill.

Up went Slick's hands – and the cake was his! He was just climbing over the hedge at the top of the hill, when Dame Toddle came panting up there, very much out of breath. She looked round for the brownie called Robin.

All she saw was Slick – and, of course, she thought he was Robin, as there was no one else about. Slick saw her too – and he thought she must be the old woman whose cake he had just taken!

"Is your name Robin?" shouted Dame Toddle. Slick heard her shouting, and to him it sounded as if she said. "Have you been robbing?" He was very much frightened and ran down the hill. Dame Toddle ran after him, waving her umbrella.

"Stop! Stop! Is your name Robin?"

"Oh dear, oh dear, I wish she'd stop shouting out that I've been robbing," said Slick. "If any one hears her they will stop me – and I'll be in prison before I can say 'Knife!' "

He ran on. Dame Toddle trotted after him too, quite determined to catch him up. "How deaf he is!" She thought to herself. "How very deaf. I must shout even more loudly this time!"

So she shouted more loudly than before.

"Stop! I say, stop! Is your name Robin? I want to speak to you."

The guilty brownie felt terribly scared.

"She says she'll get the police to me!" he groaned. "Oh dear! I'd better put down her horrid old cake and then perhaps she'll let me go."

So he popped the cake down in the newspaper and then tore off again. He climbed over the hedge and disappeared. Dame Toddle came up to the parcel in the road and undid it. When she saw a fine chocolate cake there she was most delighted.

"The kind fellow!" she thought. "I suppose he was in too much of a hurry to stop, so he left me this beautiful cake as a present! How nice of him! I don't mind having lost my sandwiches now! I'll have a piece of this cake."

So she sat down and made a good meal. Then a gnome came by wheeling a barrow, and Dame Toddle called to ask him the way to Long-way-off.

"Oh, you're nearly there," he said. "See that cottage? That's Mrs. Wags's house, the first one in the village."

"Mrs. Wags is my sister," said Dame Toddle joyfully. "Good! I have managed very well. I left my sandwiches behind – but found a lovely cake – and I've run all the way after some one to ask the way – and here he was taking me the right way all the time! It was so funny – I kept shouting after him to know if his name was Robin – but he wouldn't stop."

"*My* name's Robin," said the gnome, in surprise. "It must have been me you were looking for. I wonder who the other person was?"

"I don't know," said Dame Toddle, puzzled. "And why should he leave me a chocolate cake?"

"Goodness knows!" said Robin. "Now then – hop into my barrow, if you like, and I'll wheel you the rest of the way!"

So Dame Toddle sat in the barrow, and Robin wheeled her the rest of the way to her sister's house. How pleased she was! She gave him a piece of the chocolate cake, and then ran up the path.

"What a lucky day I've had!" she thought happily. "And now here I am at Sister Jemima's in good time for tea – and she shall have a bit of the chocolate cake too!"

So down sat the two happy old ladies – but as for that naughty brownie, he spent a very uncomfortable time indeed, for every time he met any one he felt quite certain they were going to shout, "Have you been robbing?"

And to this day he doesn't know that all Dame Toddle really wanted to know was, "Is your name Robin?"

The pink monkey had a very long tail – but do you know he had to keep it *pinned* on, because it was loose and fell off if he didn't.

Poor monkey! He was very sad about this. You see, he was a very grand monkey indeed, bright pink, with a brown nose, green eyes and paws very like hands – but his pinned-on tail spoilt him.

But what was he to do about it? He didn't want it sewn on, because he felt sure it would hurt him. He did once borrow some glue and try to stick it on – but unfortunately he got the glue all over himself, and stuck *both* ends of his tail on – one to his back and the other to his front – so that was worse than ever.

He also sat down on a piece of newspaper whilst he was trying to glue himself, and when he got up, he had stuck to the paper – so for a long time he had to walk about with sheets of paper behind him. Every one laughed till they cried – and then the golliwog kindly offered to try to get if off.

It hurt a bit – but at last the monkey was quite free of all the newspaper. The golliwog wrapped it up and was just going to throw it into the fire when the monkey gave a scream.

"Golly! You've pulled my tail away too – don't throw it into the fire!"

The golly opened the newspaper – and there was the tail all screwed up too! The monkey pounced on it and took it.

"Ooh! It nearly went into the fire. Golly, where is there a safety-pin? An ordinary pin is no use."

Golly went to Nurse's work-basket and took out a big

safety-pin. The monkey screwed himself round and pinned on his long woolly tail. He wouldn't let the golly do it
in case it hurt him.

"It's crooked," said golly.

"'Tisn't," said the monkey, trying to look over his
shoulder at his tail.

"'Tis!" said the golly.

"Well, I *like* it crooked," said monkey. But he didn't
like it crooked. He didn't like it pinned on at all. It did
spoil his beauty so. He looked quite all right from the
front – but from behind he looked dreadful – all safety-
pin and crooked tail.

One night he thought he would creep out and go to the
little old woman who lived under the hedge nearby. People
said she was very clever. The monkey felt sure she was
clever enough to fix his tail on without glue or pins.

So off he went. The moon shone down on his safety-pin
and made it very bright. He hunted about for the little old
woman, but he couldn't seem to find her house.

Then suddenly he heard a shout for help.

"Quick! Help me! Help me!"

Monkey ran on all fours to the place where the shouting came from. He was just in time to see a small elf getting up off the ground – and a frog hopping away fast
with something in his front paws.

"What's the matter?" asked the monkey.

"Oh, that horrid, horrid frog has stolen my lovely
shawl," sobbed the elf. "I shall get cold! I'm going to
a party, and I shall get so hot dancing – and then I shall
get a chill afterwards. I always do if I have no scarf or
shawl. Oh, I'm so sad!"

"Can't you go home and borrow a scarf?" said the
monkey, feeling sorry for the pretty little elf.

"My home is ever so far away," said the elf, drying
her eyes and looking at the monkey. Then she saw his

long woolly tail, which he had curled round his waist for the moment. She pointed to it.

"Oh, monkey! If you'd lend me that lovely woolly thing you've got round your waist I could wrap it round my throat and use it for a scarf. Then I wouldn't get cold."

"But that's my *tail*," said the monkey, offended.

"Oh, is it?" said the elf. "Why don't you let it go loose then? It seems funny to tie it round your waist."

"Well, I tie it round because it's only pinned on," said the monkey. "And you see, if the pin came undone I might lose my tail and not know it."

"Only *pinned* on!" shrieked the elf. "Well, unpin it then and lend it to me, can't you? It would make such a LOVELY scarf. Oh dear, darling, beautiful monkey, unpin your tail and lend it to me, do, do, do!"

The elf flung her arms round the surprised monkey – and she was so little and so sweet and so loving that he simply couldn't say no to her. So he solemnly unpinned his tail, took it off and handed it to her. The elf wrapped it round her neck and danced in delight. "It's warm, warm, warm!" she sang. "Come on, monkey darling – come with me to the party!"

And, to the pink monkey's great astonishment, the elf dragged him through the hedge – and there he was at the party! You should have seen the fairies, brownies, elves, gnomes, and pixies there! Hundreds of them, all chatting and laughing and dancing. When they saw the elf with the pink monkey they crowded round in surprise. The monkey blushed pinker than ever.

"I don't like being here without my tail," he whispered to the elf. "I don't feel dressed."

"Don't be silly!" said the elf. "Oh, listen, every one, I've had an adventure! A frog stole my shawl – and I met this monkey who had a *pinned*-on tail – and he unpinned it

"It's on!" shouted the monkey

and gave it to me for a scarf!"

"Three cheers for good old monkey!" cried all the fairies gladly, and they swung monkey round and round till he felt quite giddy. Nobody seemed to mind him not having a tail. The elf took it off when she danced and put it on a chair. Monkey kept his eyes on it, because he didn't want it to be lost. The next time the little elf put it round her neck, he went up to her and told her now he had meant to go to the little old woman who lived under the hedge and ask her to fix it on properly for him.

"Poor old monkey!" said the elf, patting his big nose. "Don't you worry about that. I know enough magic for that!"

"*Do* you!" said monkey in surprise.

"Of course!" said the elf. "Look – the party is nearly over. I can borrow a shawl to go home in. You can have your tail back – and we'll fix it on properly for you – without a pin or anything."

She clapped her hands and a dozen little folk danced up to her. She told them what she wanted, and they made a circle with the monkey in the middle. They all danced round, singing a little magic song – and then the elf threw the tail straight at monkey's back – and lo and behold, it stuck there, in exactly the right place! Fancy that!

"It's on, it's on!" shouted monkey, tugging at it in delight to make sure. "Oh, thank you a hundred times, little elf."

The elf hugged him. "You're a darling," she said. "I'm pleased to have done you a good turn. I did love wearing your warm tail for a scarf. I might come and borrow it again – you never know!"

Monkey went home as happy as could be. And *how* all the toys stared, when he showed them his tail and told them his adventures. He *was* proud of having a tail that had been a scarf, I can tell you!

Poor Mister Dawdle!

Mister Dawdle was as lazy as his name. He dawdled all day long! He got up late – he dawdled over his breakfast – he dawdled to his work – and he dawdled home again!

Mrs. Dawdle used to get so cross with him.

"Wake up, Dawdle! You're dreaming again! Hurry, hurry, hurry!"

But he wouldn't hurry.... So Mrs. Dawdle wrote to his cousin, Mister Hurry-Up, and asked him to invite Mister Dawdle to stay with him. She knew that would cure him all right!

Mister Dawdle was pleased when he got the letter from Hurry-Up, asking him to stay with him.

"That will be a nice rest for me," he said. "I shall enjoy it. I will go tomorrow. Pack my bag, dear."

So the next day Dawdle caught the bus (only just!) and arrived at the village of Quickmarch where his cousin Hurry-Up lived. What a smart village it was! Every one so neat and clean, walking about smartly. Every house nicely painted, every garden neat and trim. My word, it was a model village! Hurry-up lived in a small house, painted blue and yellow, and its knocker shone very brightly indeed.

"Hallo, hallo, hallo!" said Hurry-Up, opening the door to Dawdle. "Pleased to see you, Dawdle. Come in!"

Dawdle went in. The kitchen was neat and tidy. So was Dawdle's bedroom – very neat indeed. Dawdle thought he would never be able to keep it as neat as that!

He spent a very pleasant evening with his cousin, and then went to bed.

"Breakfast at eight o'clock sharp!" said Mr. Hurry-Up. "And don't take too long undressing, Dawdle, because candles are expensive here. Hurry yourself."

Dawdle sat down on his bed. He couldn't possibly hurry himself! Not he! He took off one sock. This took him about ten minutes – and at the end of that time Hurry-Up rushed in, blew out the candle, and said good night!

Dawdle was left in the dark! Oh dear! He couldn't see to take off his other sock, for it took him about five minutes to find his foot! He couldn't see to undo his buttons, and how he undid them he really didn't know! At last he was undressed, and somehow or other got into his pyjamas – though he put his coat sleeves on his legs, and his arms through the trousers part!

Then he tried to find the bed. He walked into the wall three times, and knocked over the wash-stand. Then he nearly walked out of the window. At last he bumped into the bed and got into it. What a relief! He drew the blankets up and didn't dawdle about going to sleep. No – he was soon snoring loudly.

At seven o'clock in the morning Mr. Hurry-Up knocked on the door. "Time to get up, Dawdle!"

Dawdle said "Oooooooph!" and fell asleep again.

At half-past seven Hurry-Up knocked again. "Getting up, Dawdle?"

"Ooooooph!" said Dawdle, and fell asleep again. At eight o'clock a most glorious smell came into the room – a smell of frying bacon, eggs, and mushrooms, a smell of new-made toast and fresh coffee! It woke Mr. Dawdle from his dreams.

A gong sounded through the house. "Dong-a-dong-dong!" There came a crash at his door. It was Mr. Hurry-Up on his way to breakfast. "Hurry! Breakfast is ready!"

Dawdle got out of bed. He was hungry – but he was so little used to hurrying that he made the silliest mistakes. He put two socks on one foot. He put his vest on over his pyjamas. He lost his braces. He put his shirt on back to front. He did his coat up all wrong. Oh dear!

At last he went down to breakfast. Only Mrs. Hurry-Up was there, looking very fierce.

"You're very late, Dawdle," she began – and then she caught sight of his appearance – one foot bare, curious-looking shirt, no collar, coat done up wrong, hair not brushed!

"Look at yourself in the glass, Dawdle," she said angrily. "Is *this* the way to come down?"

Dawdle looked at himself and blushed with horror. He fled upstairs and spent twenty minutes putting everything right. Then he came downstairs again.

The breakfast was cleared away and washed up! There wasn't a crumb to eat! Dawdle was so upset – but he didn't dare to ask for any. Just at that minute Hurry-Up came in. "Hallo, Dawdle," he said. "Had a good breakfast? My, weren't those mushrooms good? Hurry up, because we've got to catch the bus to market. It goes in ten minutes' time. We shall get our dinner in the next town. Mr. Spick-span has asked us to go to his house."

Dawdle went to find his pipe. He couldn't remember where it was. Then he found it in his pocket after all. He dawdled downstairs, filling it – and Mrs. Hurry-Up appeared from the kitchen.

"Hurry-Up told me to tell you he had started for the bus," she said. "Run, or you won't catch it! "

Dawdle was not used to running. He puffed and panted and panted and puffed – and do you know, when he reached the corner, the bus had just gone! There it was, rattling off down the lane.

"Oh my!" said Dawdle. "When does the next bus got?"

"Not for four hours," said a passer-by. "You'll have to walk. You'll get to the market by dinner-time."

Poor Dawdle set off. He simply didn't dare to go back and face Mrs. Hurry-Up. He thought he would walk all the way to the next town, ask for Mr. Spick-span's house, and join Hurry-Up there for lunch. He was really beginning to feel very hungry indeed.

He walked fast for quite a long way. Then he began to dawdle. He looked at some men mending the road. He watched some cows in a field. He looked at a train running through a tunnel. He sat down and took a stone out of his shoe.

So, by the time he reached Mr. Spick-span's house he saw Hurry-Up running down the steps, waving good-bye to Mr. Spick-span!

"Thanks for the nice dinner!" Hurry-Up was saying. "Oh, hallo, Dawdle – you didn't come to dinner after all. I wondered where you'd got to. Come on, we've got to catch the train now. I've a meeting to go to."

But this was too much for Dawdle.

"I've got a train to catch too!" he said firmly, "but it's not *your* train, Hurry-Up!"

He ran off to the station – how he ran! No dawdling about him then, for he was so afraid that Hurry-Up would catch him, and make him go to the meeting. Always hurrying, hurrying, hurrying to something!

Dawdle actually caught his train with five minutes to spare. He hid under the carriage seat till the train went out, for he was so afraid that Hurry-Up might come to look for him. Then, when the train puffed out of the station, he crawled out, much to the astonishment of two old ladies, and sat down in peace.

76

Mrs. Dawdle was so surprised to see him. "You are soon home again!" she said. "How did you get on?"

"We won't talk about it, wife," said Dawdle. "In future I will try to be quicker – but not so quick as Hurry-Up! It makes me out of breath even to think of him!"

Mrs. Dawdle smiled to herself. She could quite well guess what had happened. She didn't say anything – but whenever Dawdle is a bit lazier than usual, she says, "Oh, Dawdle – don't you think it would be nice to go and see your cousin Hurry-Up again?"

And then you should just see how Dawdles hurries with his work! You'd hardly believe it!

The Mouse and the Thimble

In Eileen's nursery the toys were very busy each night. They held a sewing-meeting, and each toy borrowed a needle from Eileen's work-basket, threaded it with cotton, and began to sew hard. They were sewing tiny flannel coats for the pixies who lived in the daffodil beds below the nursery window.

Some one had stolen the pixies' clothes whilst they were bathing in a pool of dew, and they all had dreadful colds. The toys, who were very fond of the pixies, had made up their minds to work hard, and make them warm coats. So there they sat every night, when Eileen was in bed, sewing quickly and neatly.

Only one toy grumbled about the work, and that was Benny, the blue teddy bear. He said his paws were too big to hold a needle properly.

"Don't make excuses!" said the plush duck. "*I* have no hands *or* paws to sew with, but I use one of my feet, which is much more awkward for me than you using your paw. You are lazy, Benny, that's what is the matter with you!"

The duck was quite right. Benny *was* lazy! he hated to do anything for anybody else. He liked to play about, to sing songs, and to look at his lovely collection of bright things. He had a little hidey-hole in which he kept his treasures. There were two pieces of silver paper there, a little bit of bright tin, a pearl button, the end piece of an old silver pencil and a tiny key that had once belonged to a clockwork mouse. Benny loved these bright, glittering things very much, and each night he took them out and played with them.

"Come on, Benny, you *must* do your share of sewing—" said the toys. "It's not fair. Leave your silly treasure hoard and come and get your sewing to do."

Benny went sulkily to Eileen's work-basket and took out a needle. He threaded it with cotton, and then he stood and stared in delight at something.

He had seen Eileen's new silver thimble, which her mother had bought her that day! There it shone in the basket, bright and glittering. Benny picked it up.

"Ooh!" he said to himself. "This would be a fine thing to put with my treasures!"

The naughty little bear slipped the thimble into his pocket, took up his needle and went to sew with the other toys. But after a while he got up and went to the little corner where he kept his treasures. He put the bright thimble among them, and then began playing with all the shining things.

"I shall just enjoy myself here," he thought. "Why should I go and sew every night for those silly pixies? I don't want to. I only prick my paw and I'm sure my stitches are far too big!"

He rolled the shining thimble to and fro on the floor, and watched it gleam brightly – and then a dreadful thing happened! What do you think – the thimble rolled right away, ran to a little hole in the floor-boards – and dropped down there!

The bear went to the hole and peeped down. He could quite well see the thimble shining down below. He tried to put down his paw and get it, but he couldn't. No matter now he tried he could *not* reach that thimble!

"This is terrible!" thought Benny, big tears beginning

to drop off the end of his nose. "I *must* get Eileen's thimble back. I only meant to play with it tonight, and then pop it back into her work-basket. Whatever will she say if she finds it isn't there?"

The other toys saw him crying and they came to see what the matter was. When Benny told them they were very angry with him.

"You bad bear!" they cried. "How dare you take Eileen's thimble! If you had been doing as you should have done, you would have been safely sewing with us, instead of losing a fine, silver thimble like that! However are we going to get it back?"

They tried hard to get the thimble. The duck put her beak down and tried to peck it out of the hole, but she couldn't. The clown put down his hand, but he couldn't reach the thimble. The two dolls tried as well, but nobody could get back Eileen's thimble.

"Whatever shall we do?" wept the bear.

"There's only one thing I can think of," said the golliwog, at last. "We shall have to call that little brown mouse who lives under the floor-boards, and ask her if she will kindly get us the thimble."

So they called her. She soon came, her tiny black nose twitching up and down in surprise.

"What do you want?" she asked.

"Oh, little mouse, would you be kind enough to get us that silver thimble under the boards?" asked the golliwog politely.

"I really haven't time!" said the brown mouse. "I'm just cooking my children's dinner, and after that I have to make them all new scarves to wear, because they have sore throats."

"Oh, please, oh, please!" cried the bear. "Do help me! Do, do get that thimble!"

Tears dropped off the end of Benny's nose

"Listen!" said the golliwog, suddenly. "If you will get us that thimble, brown mouse, you shall have some nice new scarves for your children. That will save you a lot of work!"

"Oh, very well," said the mouse, at once. "If you can let me have the scarves in three days' time, my children will be out of bed and ready to wear them. I have all seven in bed now, and it is very worrying, and makes a lot of work for me to do. I will get you your thimble now, and come back on Saturday for the scarves."

The mouse disappeared. The toys could hear it sniffing about below the boards, and then they heard the thimble being rolled away. Soon the mouse appeared again, with the thimble in its front paws. It pushed it out of its hole and it rolled towards the toys.

"Thank you!" they all cried. The golliwog took it and put it carefully back into Eileen's work-basket. Then he came back to the teddy bear.

"Now, Benny," he said, "you will have to work hard, won't you, if you are going to make the scarves before Saturday! Hadn't you better start?"

"What!" cried Benny. "Am I to make them all?"

"Why not?" asked the golliwog. "Wasn't it you who lost the thimble? Wasn't it because you were lazy that all this happened? Well, you must pay for your laziness now. Get your needle and cotton and set to work."

The bear looked round at the toys. They were all looking very sternly at him, and he felt afraid. He knew he would have to do as he was told. The duck looked as if she was going to peck him. The two dolls seemed ready to slap him and the clown was more than ready to pinch the fat, lazy little bear!

Benny took up his needles and cotton, and began to sew the piece of blue flannel that the golliwog gave him. It was a long piece, shaped like a scarf, and it had to be neatly hemmed down the sides and along the ends. The stitches had to be small, and the bear found it very difficult. He kept pricking his fat paws, and the tears fell down his hairy nose again. But the toys took no notice. They all thought it was a very good punishment for the lazy little bear.

That night he finished one scarf. The next night he made two. The next night he made two again, and how he had to work!

"Hurry!" the toys said. "The mouse is coming tomorrow night, and you still have two more scarves to finish!"

"Oh, I do wish I'd never been lazy!" groaned the bear. "I should be able to sew much more quickly, if only I'd done my sewing each night with you. I shall never, never be lazy again. I have far more sewing to do now than ever I should have had if I'd only shared your work with you!"

"Well," said the golliwog, at once, "If you really *are* sorry, Benny, we'll help you – but mind – you must never be lazy again! Lazy people always find that they have far more work to do in the end, you know, just as you have found!"

The toys set to work to help Benny, who was very grateful. Soon the last two scarves were finished, and laid out ready for the little brown mouse.

When she came, she was delighted. There were two blue scarves, two green, two yellow and one pink.

"My small mice will be *so* pleased!" said the brown mouse, her nose twitching very fast indeed. "They are all up again now, and I want to take them out for a walk tomorrow. They can wear their new scarves. Thank you very much."

She ran off with the scarves, and the toys could hear

squeaks of delight as she showed them to her tiny brown children. Benny felt pleased.

"Well, it *is* nice to give such pleasure to any one!" he said. "I'm glad I had to work hard at those scarves now. I won't be lazy and selfish again. I do understand how nice it is to work for some one else. Thank you, toys, for helping me."

"You're a good little fellow at heart," said the golliwog, and he hugged the fat bear. "We were sorry to have punished you. Now let's all go and have a game – we've done enough sewing this week!"

So off they all went to have a game of hide-and-seek, and you should have heard their squeals of delight! The loudest squeals of all came from Benny the bear. He was *so* pleased to be friends with every one again!

The Little Soldier

Once there was a little toy soldier. He was dressed in red, and once he had carried a gun, but that had got broken off. He stood up very straight, and wore a black bearskin on his head, which made him look very grand.

He belonged to Ronnie. Ronnie had found him right at the very, very bottom of his Christmas stocking, and he was fond of the little red soldier. He called him "Redman", and always carried him about everywhere because he was sure he was lucky.

Redman liked being in Ronnie's pocket. There were marbles to talk to, and sometimes a bit of toffee to lick. There was a little hole in the pocket too, and Redman could just see nicely out of it if he lay down on his side and peeped out. Sometimes Ronnie stood Redman out on the table to see everything that was going on. Often he put him into his clockwork train, and then Redman would go whirling round and round the lines until he felt so giddy that he couldn't stand up, and had to fall down with a bang!

One morning Ronnie took Redman into the kitchen. His mother was there, making a big fruit cake. Ooooh! The things she put into that fruit cake – currants, raisins, sultanas, bits of nut, bits of candied peel – it was going to be the finest cake that ever was! Ronnie climbed up on a chair and watched his mother in delight.

"Mother, can I scrape the dish round when the mixing is finished?" he asked. "I do like the taste of all the bits!"

"Yes," said Mother, stirring away. "Don't lean over the basin like that, Ronnie. If you fall in, it would be so difficult to separate you from the bits!"

"Mother, Redman would like to see you making this lovely cake!" said Ronnie. He felt in his pocket and put Redman on the table. Redman had been peeping out of the hole in the pocket, so he had already seen what was happening, but he was very pleased indeed to see things properly. He stood on the table, trying his hardest to make himself tall enough to see what was in the basin.

"Redman can't see into the basin," said Ronnie. "I'll stand him on this tin here, Mother. Then he can see all you do."

So he stood Redman on a big tin by the basin, and Redman had a fine view of all the currants, raisins, sultanas, bits of nuts, and bits of peel, to say nothing of the flour and the sugar and eggs. My, it was a wonderful sight, and the smell of the basin was glorious! Ronnie wished his mother would hurry up and put the cake into the oven – then he could scrape out the dish!

Just then the butcher came to the door. Ronnie ran to open it. "Wait a minute," said Mother, wiping her hands, "I want to pay the bill."

Now whilst she was paying the bill, and Ronnie was at the door, watching the pennies and the shillings going into the butcher's purse, an awful thing happened to Redman. He toppled over – he tried to save himself by clutching at the tin – he couldn't, he couldn't! And down, down, down he fell into the basin of cake-mixture – all among the currants, raisins, sultanas, and the rest!

He scrambled about, trying to get out, but he couldn't. It was too sticky! Poor little Redman!

Mother came back to the table. She took up her spoon and began to stir again, round and round – and poor Redman disappeared into the cake-mixture. Round and round he went, and his red body became covered with currants, sultanas, bits of nut and peel. Whatever was he to do? He called out, hoping that Ronnie would hear him – but

86

his voice was smothered in the mixture.

"Mother, where's my Redman?" asked Ronnie, a few minutes later.

"I haven't any idea!" said Mother. "He was on the tin just now!"

Ronnie looked all over the table for him. He hunted on the floor. He felt in his pockets. No Redman to be found anywhere! He was very sad.

"Mother, I *must* find Redman!" he said. "I love him you know. He brings me luck." He was almost crying.

"Don't be a baby, Ronnie," said Mother, stirring away. "He'll turn up some time! I expect you've dropped him somewhere."

"But I never *do* drop him," said Ronnie.

"Get out of my way for a minute," said Mother. "I want to put my cake in the oven."

She put the mixture into a big tin. She carried the tin to the oven, and popped it inside.

My goodness gracious, the oven *was* hot. Redman, buried deep in the cake mixture, felt himself getting hotter and hotter. He wished he could take the big bearskin off his head. He wished he could undo his coat. He wished – he wished – oh, he wished lots of lovely cool things, and all the time he got hotter, and hotter, and HOTTER!

"I'm cooking with the cake," he said. "I'm cooking with the cake! What shall I be like when I'm cooked! I shall be eaten! Oh, I am a most unlucky little soldier!"

The cake cooked for two long hours. Redman had got so hot that he couldn't even think. He felt that he was just a bit of cake. At last Mother opened the oven door and dug a fork into the cake to see if it was done.

"Nicely baked!" she said, in joy, and took the cake out of the oven. She put it in on a shelf to cool. Ronnie looked at it, but he didn't even smile when he saw it. He was still unhappy about Redman!

87

"Cheer up, Ronnie," said Mother. Ronnie said, in a little sad voice, "I shan't want any cake till I've found Redman again! You don't know how I miss him in my pocket."

"Well, I do know you're a silly little boy, grumbling and groaning!" said Mother, who was quite sure Redman would turn up again somewhere. "Nobody's eaten Redman, have they? Well then, he must be somewhere!"

"But he *isn't* somewhere!" said Ronnie. "I've looked simply everywhere, Mother!"

Mother sent him out to play for a time. When he came in it was tea-time. Redman knew it was tea-time, too, for he heard Mother getting the tea ready. He heard the kettle boiling – it sang its usual little song. He heard Ronnie taking off his boots. He was deep inside the cake, feeling very much cooler – but now he was terribly afraid of being eaten!

"They don't know I'm here!" he said to himself. "They'll eat me! I'll be bitten in two! Oh, my goodness!"

Mother put the big fruit cake on a plate and set it in the middle of the table. It did look fine! Ronnie simply couldn't help feeling hungry when he saw it. He ate his bread and butter and then looked at the cake.

"Well, do you feel you could eat a little of this nice new cake after all?" said Mother, smiling. "Or do you still feel too bad about Redman?"

"I do still feel bad about him," said Ronnie. "But I'd like a bit of cake all the same, Mother."

Mother cut a big piece of cake – and oh dear, oh *dear*, Redman was in the slice she cut! He was – all mixed up with currants and things. Mother put the slice on to Ronnie's plate. It *was* a big one. Ronnie was pleased.

He took a bite and chewed it up. He took another bite – a very big one – and his teeth met on something hard. He bit on it – how funny – it wasn't nut, whatever could it be?

Ronnie put his mouthful out on to his plate. His mother looked at him crossly. "What a way to behave, Ronnie!" she said.

"But, Mother, there's something big and hard there," said Ronnie. "Oh! oh! Mother! Mother! Look, it's Redman! Redman is in the cake! Mother, you *cooked* Redman! He's in the cake – and I nearly ate him! Oh, poor little Redman!"

Mother laughed and laughed. "Well," she said, "it's the first time I've cooked a soldier in a cake. He must have fallen off his tin into the basin! Oh, Ronnie, how funny that you should have had the slice where Redman was."

"Oh, I'm so happy!" said Ronnie. "Mother, can I go and wash him? He doesn't like all this cake on him. Oh, do you suppose I hurt him when I bit him?"

"Not a bit," said Mother, still laughing. "Go and wash him if you like."

Ronnie washed him – and then stood Redman just beside his plate, so that he could see everything. The little boy was so happy again to have found his lucky toy soldier. As for Redman, he was very happy too! What a tale he would have to tell the things in Ronnie's pocket!

"I've been mixed – and cooked – and nearly eaten!" he said proudly. "I am a most remarkable soldier!"

Well, he had a most remarkable adventure, didn't he! All the same, it's not an adventure I would like for myself – would you?

Tinker-dog and Prince

Tinker-dog lived with his master in a little tumbledown cottage at the end of Tiptop Village. He wasn't a terrier, and he wasn't a collie, and he wasn't a spaniel. I couldn't tell you what he was – he just wasn't anything but a plain dog. But his master loved him and called him a fine fellow.

Prince was a beautiful Alsatian dog, so like a grand wolf that you could hardly tell he wasn't. He was worth a lot of money, and he was as proud as could be. He waked along the road as if it belonged to him, and if he met Tinker-dog he growled at him angrily.

"Growl away, Prince High and Mighty!" Tinker barked back. "I can race you any day, though you run like the wind! My legs are as good as yours!"

"Common little dog!" said Prince, in his deep growly voice. "Keep out of my way. I am a prize dog. I win prizes at shows. You wouldn't win a prize at all – except for the ugliest, commonest dog in the show. Woooooooof!"

Tinker-dog ran home. He was sometimes a bit sad because he knew quite well he *was* a common little dog, and would certainly never win a prize at any show. He didn't want a prize for himself – but it would be so nice to win a prize for his master, whom he loved very much!

Now one day Prince and Tinker met by the river.

"Woooooooof!" said Prince, snarling at Tinker-dog. "Why don't ou keep out of my way? I don't like your looks. I don't like your smell. I don't like your . . ."

"I don't like your *manners*!" said Tinker, and he actually bit the end of Prince's tail! What would have happened next I don't know – but, just at that moment, a little boy who was playing by the river, suddenly gave a scream and fell right into the water!

"Help! Help!" shouted the other children. Prince stared at the water. Tinker-dog stared too and barked to Prince. "You are a big strong dog. Jump in and pull the little boy out!"

But Prince ran away! It was Tinker-dog who jumped into the cold water and swam bravely to the little boy. He caught hold of the child's coat and then turned back to the bank. How heavy the little boy was! Tinker-dog puffed and panted, but he didn't let go! He struggled on and on.

"Look at that good little dog!" suddenly cried a man's voice. "He's got the child safely! Come on – let's help him!"

But Tinker needed no help. Just at that moment he reached the bank, and the little boy, spluttering and choking, climbed out, pulled by the other children.

"Brave dog! Good dog!" cried all the watching people, for there was now quite a crowd by the river. "Who is he? Why, he is the little dog belonging to Mr. Brown!"

Tinker-dog didn't know what all the fuss was about. He shook himself well and ran off home.

"Brave dog! Good dog!" every one shouted after him. And then some one said, "I saw that great big Alsatian dog called Prince run away! *He* didn't rescue Tommy! He was a coward – he ran away and left the job to a dog three times as small as himself! Tinker-dog deserves a medal!"

Soon the news about Tinker-dog was all round the town! A newspaperman came to see Tinker-dog's master and took Tinker's photograph! It was in the paper next morning and underneath Tinker's picture was put:

"The finest dog in our town. Tinker-dog, who saved little Tommy from the river! What shall we give him for reward?"

Now the next week there was a dog show in the town, and, of course, Prince was going, for he hoped to win the best prizes. And do you know, a man came to Tinker-dog's master and asked him to take Tinker too.

"He won't win a prize for being a beautiful dog," he said, "but the dog-show people want to give him a medal and a fine red collar because he is the bravest dog they know. Little Tommy is to give it to him."

So Tinker-dog, much to his surprise, was taken to the show, nicely washed and brushed. Prince went too – and when he saw Tinker-dog he laughed and said, "Fancy you turning up at my show, Tinker! Coming to see me take all the prizes?"

"Hullo, funny-face!" said Tinker-dog, and ran along beside his master.

Prince did win a prize – but, oh dear, what do you suppose he felt like, when at the end of the show, he saw the chief judge got up on to the platform and call for Tinker-dog.

"Now we come to the most important dog in the town!" said the judge, patting Tinker, who wagged his tail and looked most surprised. "This is Tinker-dog, who saved little Tommy from drowning last week. Prince, the big prize Alsatian, was by the river too – but he ran away! It was little dog Tinker that jumped into the water! Three cheers for Tinker-dog!"

"Hip-hip-hip-hurrah!" shouted every one. And then, up to the platform walked little Tommy, carrying a fine red collar with a silver medal hanging from it!

He put the collar round Tinker's neck. How the medal shone and glittered when Tinker wagged his stumpy tail!

Tinker-dog caught hold of the child's coat

He was the happiest dog in the world. His master was sitting nearby, looking so pleased, and proud of his dog. Tinker wuffed to him. "I've won a prize for you, master! I may be a common little dog, but I've done something after all!"

Every one went home talking of Tinker-dog. Prince went home too, drooping his tail. What did it matter winning a prize for being splendid and beautiful to look at? Nobody looked at him – every one wanted to see Tinker, that common little dog! Prince sat by the fire and thought and thought.

"It isn't good looks that matter after all, or even good manners!" he thought to himself. "It is good deeds. I must tell Tinker when I see him."

So the next time he saw Tinker he ran over to him. "Tinker-dog, I may be a grand-looking dog, but you are a better dog than I am," he said. "I'd like to be friends with you, if you'll let me."

"Wuff-wuff! Of course," said Tinker. "Pleased to go for a walk with you any day, Prince!"

And now the two are always seen together, and perhaps one day Prince will be able to show that he can be as brave as Tinker – what do *you* think?

Twiddley-bit's Punishment

Twiddley-Bit was a mouse – and he was not at all a good mouse. He was greedy, rather deceitful, and very untruthful. So he wasn't very often asked out to tea, as you can imagine.

One night Mrs. Whiskers gave a party. It was to be a cheese-party, for Mrs. Whiskers had discovered a very fine cheese sitting on a shelf in the dairy.

She asked six mice to her party. There were Tailer, Sniffy, Woffly, Patter, Four-Paws, and Squeak – but not Twiddley-Bit.

He was angry. He met Tailer, and Tailer said to him, "Are you going to Mrs. Whiskers's party?" and he had to say no. He met Sniffy, and Sniffy said to him, "Are you going to Mrs. Whiskers's party?" and he again had to say no. Then he met Woffly, Patter, Four-Paws, and Squeak, and they all said to him, "Are you going to Mrs. Whiskers's party?" and he had to say no four times.

Then they all said, "Why not?" And Twiddley-Bit didn't know what to answer. He couldn't very well say, "Because I am a greedy, deceitful mouse and nobody likes me!" could he?

He ran off to his hole, feeling cross and spiteful. "I'll spoil their party somehow – and get the cheese for myself!" he thought. "Yes, I will! I'll show them that they can't leave me out of things!"

So that night, when he saw Mrs. Whiskers and the rest going off to the cheese-party, all dressed in their best bows, he crept after them. When he saw the cheese he nearly fell off the shelf with surprise and delight. *What* a cheese!

He had a very simple plan. He meant to jump out at the mice, crying, "Cat! Beware the cat! She is in the dairy! Cat, cat, cat!" Then he knew all the mice would rush away – and Twiddley-Bit would eat the cheese himself. What a joke!

He did just what he had planned to do. He leapt out from behind the cheese, and squeaked loudly. "Cat! Beware the cat! She is in the dairy! Cat, cat, cat!"

"Ee! EEE! EE!" squealed the frightened mice, and they ran for their holes in a trice. Twiddley-Bit was left alone by the cheese. How his little black eyes shone! He began to nibble – and nibble – and nibble!

And then a dreadful thing happened to him. A big paw came down on him – he was caught by the cat, who really *had* been in the dairy after all, watching for mice!

"Eeeeeeee!" squeaked Twiddley-Bit in fright. "Let me go!"

"You're the mouse who frightened all the other mice I was waiting for!" said the cat. "If it hadn't been for you I would have caught the lot! Well – I've got *you*, at any rate!"

"Eeeeeeee!" squealed Twiddley-Bit. "I didn't know you were there!"

"I'm going to eat you!" said the cat. And there is no doubt at all that she meant what she said – but suddenly something happened. A jug of milk that stood on the shelf above, overturned, and a stream of milk poured down on the cat's head. She jumped in fright and let Twiddley-Bit go. He darted into a hole at once and crouched there, trembling.

"*We* upset the milk on the cat and saved you!" said Mrs. Whiskers, running up to the frightened little mouse. "I am glad you are safe."

"But – but – but – why did you save me?" stammered Twiddley-Bit. "I deceived you – I told you an untruth, or thought I did – I wanted all that cheese for myself. Why did you bother about a horrid, nasty little mouse like me?"

"Oh, well," said Mrs. Whiskers, "because *you* are horrid and nasty is no reason why *we* should be, Twiddley-Bit. It's no use being unkind just because somebody else is. We don't want to be as horrid as you, you know."

Twiddley-Bit crept away, ashamed. He had been unkind and horrid, but the others had not been the same. They had saved his life. He would never, never, never forget it!

He didn't forget it. He is a nice little mouse now, and always goes to every party there is – so you can guess he turned over a new leaf that night!

Peter's Fire-engine

Peter had seen the fire-engine go down the street. What a splendid sight it was! The firemen wore their glittering helmets, the fire-engine was bright and shining, and the bell clanged loudly as the fire brigade tore along.

"Clang! Clang! Clang!"

All the cars hurried out of the way. People stood still on the pavement. Nobody crossed the road when the fire-engine tore by!

Mother watched it with Peter. They stood at the front gate. "When I was a little girl the fire-engine was pulled by galloping horses," said Mother. "They raced down the street, and their hoofs went clip-clop and the bell rang dong-ding-dong! I wish you could have seen the horses, Peter."

"Oh, Mother! I shall make a fire-engine of my own!" said Peter, excited. "I shall make Tony be the horse – he is a good dog and loves to play horses with me. And my little cart shall be the fire-engine!"

Peter ran off. He got out his cart. It was big enough for him to sit in. It had two long handles, and Peter often pulled it by these. He ran to find Tony.

"Tony! Tony! Where are you? Come and play fire-engines!"

Tony ran up, wagging his tail. He was a fine dog for playing. He would do anything. Peter stood him between the handles of the cart and tied reins to his collar and knotted them to the handles.

"Now what about a bell?" said Peter. "Mother! Can I have the kitchen bell – the one you ring when you want me to come in to dinner?"

Mother said yes – so Peter fetched it. It was a fine big one and said, "Ding-a-dong-a-ding-a-dong-a!" when Peter shook it.

Peter's cart had a little arch of wood at the front, and Peter tied the bell to the middle of this so that it hung down loosely. It would ring as soon as the cart moved! What fun!

"Now my fire-engine is ready!" said Peter. "I must be a fireman now. What shall I have for a helmet?"

He remembered that Daddy had an old bowler hat hanging up in the hall. That would do well! Then he found the axe belonging to his Red Indian suit and fastened that to his side.

"If I have to hack down doors to save people my axe will come in useful," he said. He looked fine in the bowler hat.

"Now I must wait for a fire!" he said. So he waited. He jumped up suddenly and shouted loudly.

"Fire! Fire! I see a fire! There is a house on fire! I must go and put it out! Oh dear! Where's the water? I've forgotten that!"

He ran to the shed and got a watering-can. He filled it with water and put it in his cart. There wasn't room for him in the cart, too, so he thought he had better run by the side.

"Now we're ready!" he shouted. "Fire! Here comes the fire-engine! I'll soon put out the fire! Here comes the fire-engine! Gee-up, Tony!"

Tony ran off, dragging the cart behind him. The bell shook and rang loudly. "Ding-a-dong-a-ding-a-dong-a-ding!

99

Off went the fire-engine round the garden! Tony galloped at full speed, the bell rang, Peter shouted, and the water splashed out of the can into the cart! My goodness, it *was* fun!

Peter stopped, quite out of breath.

"The only thing is," he said, "there isn't *really* a fire!"

And just then – my goodness – he saw a fire! Yes, he really did! It was in the next-door garden. Mr. Brown lived there, and he had lighted a bonfire to burn his rubbish – and what do you think! The flames had reached out to the fence and were burning it!

"Fire! Fire! Fire!" yelled Peter, in great excitement. "*Really* a fire! Gallop, Tony! Gallop!"

Tony galloped. He flew down the path and out into the road. The bell rang ding-a-ding! Peter turned Tony into the gate next door, and together they raced down to the bottom of the garden there.

"Fire! Here we come, the finest fire-engine in the world! We'll soon put out the fire! Here come the brave firemen!"

The fire-engine came to a stop by the burning fence. Peter lifted the watering-can out of the cart. He tilted it over the flames.

"Sizzle-sizzle-sizzle!" The flames died right down – the fence was saved! Only a little bit had been burnt right away!

Mr. Brown came running down the garden.

"Good gracious!" he said, "I *was* in a way when I saw my fence burning! Thank you, Peter, for putting out the fire. You *are* a good boy!"

"Well, you see, I happened to be a fireman this morning," said Peter. "So it was lucky for me there was a real fire!"

"And how lucky for me there was a firemen and a fine fire-engine and horse so near!" said Mr. Brown. "Would

Peter tilted the watering-can over the flames

the fireman come in and have some cake and lemonade, do you think?"

"Oh yes," said Peter. "Firemen are always hungry after a fire!"

So he went indoors and had two slices of ginger cake and a glass of lemonade. It was lovely! Tony had a bone, because, Mr. Brown said, he deserved something too.

"It *has* been a lovely morning!" Peter said to Mother, when he got home. "It isn't often a pretend comes real, Mother, is it?"

"It certainly isn't!" said Mother.

Tiddley-pom's Pencil

Tiddley-Pom the tailor was very happy. The King had given him a beautiful gold pencil with his name on, because the little tailor had made him a splendid red party suit.

"Look!" Tiddley-Pom said to every one he met. "Look! See my beautiful golden pencil! The King gave it to me!"

Tiddley-Pom's wife was very pleased. She took a good look at the pencil and said, "Now, Tiddley-Pom, you just be careful with this pencil. You know how careless you are with your things – always putting them down here, there, and everywhere, and never being able to find them again. Just choose a safe place for your pencil, and keep it there when you are not using it."

"In my pocket?" said Tiddley-Pom.

"No," said his wife. "That's a silly place, because your pockets always have holes."

"You should mend them," said Tiddley-Pom.

"I do," said Mrs. Tiddley-Pom, "but you will keep putting your scissors into them, Tiddley-Pom, and the points make holes."

"I'll keep my pencil on the mantelpiece," said Tiddley-Pom.

"No," said his wife. "It might roll off there."

"Well," said the tailor. "I'll tie it on a bit of string and tie the string to a button on my coat! What do you think of that, wife?"

"No good at all," said Mrs. Tiddley-Pom. "You are always taking your coat off – and you forget where you leave it, so your pencil would be gone too! Do you know,

Tiddley-Pom, that I found your coat on the *roof* the other day. Now how *did* it get there?"

"It must have been left there when I went up to watch the sweep's brush coming out of the chimney!" said the tailor going red. "Oh, wife! I know such a good place! I'll keep my pencil behind my ear – like this!"

He stuck the lovely gold pencil behind his ear, and it stayed there nicely, because Tiddley-Pom had great big pointed ears, and only the tip of the pencil could be seen sticking out.

"That's quite a good place," said his wife. "Now I'm going out shopping, Tiddley. So get on with your work whilst I'm gone."

Off she went. Tiddley-Pom settled down to his sewing very happily. He whistled as he worked, and a good many of his friends came and chatted with him at the open window. One of them was old Dame Tubby, who had been away a week with her sister.

"I hear the King gave you a beautiful gold pencil, Tiddley-Pom," she said. "Will you show it to me?"

"Oh, haven't you seen it?" said the tailor. "I'll love to show it to you."

He put his hands into his pocket to get the pencil. It wasn't there.

"Funny!" said Tiddley-Pom. "I usually keep my pencil there. Wait a minute. I may have put it on the mantelpiece."

He ran to the mantelpiece. No pencil there either. Tiddley-Pom scratched his head and thought.

"It must be *somewhere* about!" he said. "I had it about half an hour ago."

"Perhaps it has been stolen," said Dame Tubby. "A valuable pencil like that might easily be stolen, you know. A witch or a gnome would be pleased to have it!"

"Ooh!" said Tiddley-Pom in alarm. "So they might.

Oh, Dame Tubby, Snippy the gnome came in this morning – and Witch Toddles – and the Yellow Witch too – and Higgle the gnome as well! Do you suppose any of them took it?"

"Well, I shouldn't think so," said Dame Tubby. "They are all friends of yours, aren't they? *I'll* tell you what to do, Tiddley-Pom. I've got a spell at home for robbers. I'll go and get it. Wait a minute. We'll soon get back your pencil!"

Dame Tubby ran off. On the way home she told every one about Tiddley-Pom's lost pencil, and how she was getting a spell to find the robber. So, before she had got back to the shop again, about twenty gnomes, goblins, witches, fairies, and pixies had arrived at Tiddley-Pom's, all anxious to hear the latest news of the wonderful pencil.

Dame Tubby came back, most important. In her hand she carried a little box. "Look, Tiddley-Pom," she said. "There's a yellow powder in here. Blow it into the air, and call upon it to find the one who has the pencil."

"But how shall I know who has it?" asked Tiddley-Pom.

"Oh, you must choose something that the spell makes them do," said Dame Tubby, excited. "Tell the spell to start them braying like a donkey – or standing on their head – or galloping like a horse! Then as soon as the spell begins to work, we'll see which of us is doing that, and we'll find the pencil on him!"

"Ooh!" said Tiddley-Pom, "it's a powerful spell. I know what I'll do. I'll tell it to make the robber quack like a duck and hop on one foot all the way down the street. Then we shall soon find the one who has my beautiful gold pencil."

Tiddley-Pom took the box, and opened the lid. He blew the powder up into the air, crying, "Spell, spell, find the one who has my pencil! Make him quack like a duck and hop all the way down the street! "

The powder flew up into the air with a queer crackling noise and disappeared.

Every one stood still and looked at every one else. Who was the thief? Nobody moved – and then, suddenly, a most peculiar thing happened!

Tiddley-Pom began to quack! You should have heard him!

"Quarck, quarck, quarck!" he said, opening and shutting his mouth like a beak. "Quarck, quarck, quarck, quarck!"

And then he put up one leg and began to hop solemnly to the door – and out of it – and down the street! All the time he quarcked very loudly; it did sound so funny! "Quarck, quarck, quarck, quarck, quarck, quarck, quarck!"

Every one stared in amazement. The spell must have gone wrong! Down the street hopped Tiddley-Pom – and whom should he meet at the corner but his wife, coming back from her shopping! When she saw Tiddley-Pom hopping along, quacking for all he was worth, she nearly fell over!

"Tiddley-Pom! What is the meaning of this?" she cried.

"Quarch, quarck!" said Tiddley.

"Don't quarck, quarck at me!" said Mrs. Tiddley-Pom angrily. "What are you behaving in this foolish manner for?"

"Quarck, quarck, quarck, quarck!" said Tiddley, and went on hopping. His wife took hold of him and shook him angrily.

"Quarck, quarck," said Tiddley sadly, and then as his wife shook him again, something flew out from behind his ear and fell on the ground! It was his pencil! He had put it behind his ear for safety, you remember – and had forgotten all about it!

"Quarck, quarck!" cried Tiddley joyfully, and picked it up. Then every one rushed up and began to explain things to Mrs. Tiddley-Pom. How surprised she was! She took hold of Tiddley-Pom by the collar and walked him home, though he still tried to hop, and quacked loudly all the way.

"You'll just go to bed until you stop quacking!" she said to him. "And I hope that after this you will try to remember where you put things! Hopping and quacking indeed, trying to find your pencil, and it's behind your ear all the time. You're a donkey, Tiddley-Pom, and you should bray, not quack!"

Well, Tiddley got better after a few days – but if he loses anything now, he gets very flustered, and begins to quack! It's funny to hear him.

"Quarck, quarck, quarck!" he says – and you may be sure Mrs. Tiddley-Pom comes rushing out to see what he has lost.

The Very Clever Kite

Timothy was so excited. Mummy was going to take him to see a conjurer at the Town Hall, and it was said that he could really do the most marvellous things imaginable! He could put water into a teapot, and when it poured out, it was cocoa!

And then, by waving his handkerchief over the cup of cocoa, he could turn it into a bowl with a goldfish swimming about. Just imagine that!

So it was no wonder that Timothy was excited. He kept thinking and thinking and thinking about the conjurer, and he was so pleased and happy that he simply could *not* sit still for a moment!

It was a very windy day. The trees sang a song as they swung their branches about. The smoke from the chimneys twisted this way and that like witches' cloaks, and the flag on the flag-mast at the bottom of the garden flapped as if it had wings!

There came a knock at the door. Mummy went to it, and there was the laundry man, with the basket of clean linen.

"Wait a moment," said Mummy. "I will pay you."

She ran to get her bag, and took a pound note out of it. Just as she was handing it to the man, a dreadful thing happened. The wind suddenly blew by in a terrific gust and snatched the note out of Mummy's hand. In a trice it was blown away, high in the air, and flew right over the hedge, and was lost to sight!

"Oh!" cried Mummy, in dismay. "Quick! Let's look for it! Timothy! Come and help!"

Well, they all hunted and hunted and hunted – but not

a sign of that pound note could they see! It might have blown as far as the next village, for all they knew.

Mummy went sadly back to the house.

"Timothy, I can't take you to the conjurer's now," she said. "I am so very sorry. But I've no more money."

Timothy was dreadfully disappointed. He wanted to cry – but when he saw his mother looking so upset he knew that he must pretend not to care, so that she wouldn't feel even more unhappy. So he gave her a hug, and said, "Never mind, Mummy! *I* don't mind about the conjurer! Don't you worry about *me*!"

Wasn't that nice of him? He went and put on his hat and coat to go and tell his friend Jimmy that he would not be going to see the conjurer now, and to ask Jimmy if he would be sure to remember everything to tell him, if *he* went.

"Jimmy's out in the field flying his kite," said Jimmy's mother. So Timothy ran to the field and sure enough there was Jimmy, flying his kite high in the air. What a wind there was! The little boys could hardly hear themselves speak!

"The kite can't go any higher!" said Jimmy. "I've used every single inch of string!"

"I hope the string won't break," said Timothy anxiously. "The kite is pulling very hard!"

And do you know, *just* as he spoke, the string *did* break! Wasn't it dreadful? It broke a little way up in the air – and the kite at once flew away, dragging its long tail and its string behind it!

"Oh!" cried Jimmy, in dismay. "My lovely kite! It's gone!"

The two boys watched it. It dipped down suddenly, then dipped again and disappeared behind a tree.

"Quick!" said Timothy. "We may get it if we hurry. Perhaps it is caught somewhere."

The boys raced over the field, climbed over the wall at the end, and found themselves in a little wood. They hunted anxiously for the kite, and could not see it anywhere.

"It's too bad!" said Timothy. "This horrid wind! It blew away my Mummy's money today so that she can't take me to see the conjurer – and now it's taken away your kite!"

They went on hunting – and suddenly Timothy gave a shout, and pointed upwards.

"Look! It's up there! Caught in that tree!"

"Oh dear! I can't climb *that* tree," said Jimmy. "I'd be afraid of falling."

"Well, *I'll* climb it and get the kite," said Timothy. "I'm used to climbing. I'm always climbing the trees in our garden at home."

So up he went. It was very difficult. A branch caught at his leg and scratched it. A big twig struck into his cheek and pricked him. But up he went – and at last he reached the kite. He pulled it free from the branch it had fallen on, and was just about to go down again when he saw a big hole in the tree. "I wonder if there's a nest there," he thought, and slipped his hand in.

There was a nest – but it was a very old one, falling to pieces. There was something that rustled in the nest. Timothy thought it was a dead leaf. He pulled it out to see.

But when he saw what it was he got such a surprise that he *very* nearly fell right out of the tree! It was the pound note his mother had lost! Yes, it was, really!

"The wind must have blown it all the way across the field, into the tree – and it must have slipped into the hole!" cried Timothy. "Oh, Jimmy, Jimmy, what luck! Now Mummy will be able to take me to see the conjurer after all. Hurrah!"

It was the pound note his mother had lost

"Hurrah!" cried Jimmy, too, pleased to see his friend's excited face. "Throw down the kite, Timothy. We'll race home and tell your mother."

They tore off – and Timothy's mother was *so* pleased and excited. She hugged both little boys, and heard the story of how the kite got caught in the tree, again, and again, and again.

"We'll go to see the conjurer and we'll take Jimmy with us, as it was his kite that so kindly found my money for me!" she laughed.

"Wasn't it a *clever* kite!" said Jimmy, full of joy to think that he was going to have such a treat.

Well, they all went to see the conjurer that afternoon, and didn't they have fun! Do you know, the conjurer took a shilling out of Jimmy's left ear, and a rabbit out of Timothy's cap. It was really most astonishing!

"I don't think I've ever seen a cleverer thing!" said Jimmy, as they went home.

"Except your kite!" said Timothy. "That was even cleverer than the conjurer, Jimmy! It found a pound note in a bird's nest instead of an egg!"

The Golliwog and the Canary

In Emma's nursery lived her toys – and her little yellow canary, called Goldie. He was a dear little fellow, and sang loudly whenever the sun shone on his cage.

One night Goldie the canary was very unhappy – for what do you think? Emma had forgotten to give him any seed that day, and he had no fresh water! Wasn't it a pity? Poor Goldie was very sad. Emma had never forgotten him before. He was hungry and thirsty. He had bathed in his drinking-water the day before, so there was hardly any left.

He sat and moped in his cage after Emma had gone to bed. He watched the toys creep out from their cupboard to play. They were excited because they were planning a dance, and they were going to ask the two small fairies to come, who lived outside the window in the old apple tree. What fun!

"Hie, Goldie, what's the matter?" suddenly called the golliwog. "You look very miserable."

"So I am," said Goldie, with a tiny twitter. "I've no seed and no water. I'm hungry and thirsty – and I've got to go all through the night till the morning without anything to eat or drink."

"What a shame!" said the golliwog. "Can't I give you some, Goldie? Tell me where the seed-tin is."

"It's over there in that little cupboard," said the canary joyfully. "Oh, do you think you could find it and open it and give me some, Golly?"

"I think so," said the golliwog, and he ran to the cupboard. He found the tin and opened it. Inside were the little seeds that the canary ate. The golly got a tiny plate from Emma's tea-set in the toy cupboard, and dipped it into the tin. He took the plateful of seed to the window-sill, climbed up the curtain there, and reached the canary's cage, where it hung by the window. He emptied the seed into the canary's seed-tin. How pleased Goldie was!

He pecked and pecked at the seed, and had a very good dinner. Then he wanted a drink very badly. The golly looked round and wondered how he could give him one. Then a good idea came into his head.

Emma had a toy garden in the cupboard – and there was a tiny watering-can that belonged to it – a very tiny one indeed. The golly would fill it with water and then pour it out into Goldie's water-dish! Good!

But where was the water? There seemed to be none in the nursery. Ah – what about the water in the goldfish globe? That would do well. The goldfish could easily spare a tiny canful. The golly climbed up to the bookshelf on top of which was a globe, and asked the fish if he might take a little water.

He filled the tiny can, climbed down again, and then climbed up to the cage. He tipped up the can, put the spout between the wires – and pitter-patter, pitter-patter the water poured into the dish! Then the canary had a good drink – and didn't he enjoy it!

"That's very kind of you," he said to the golly. "Thanks very much."

The golly smiled all over his kind black face and went back to the other toys, who were still planning excitedly what they were going to do at the dance the next night.

"What music shall we have?" asked the teddy.

"The musical box, of course!" said the pink rabbit. "It only needs winding up now and then – it goes on for a lovely long time — and we can dance to the music beautifully."

"Good!" said the teddy. "Well, I'll go and ask the two fairies now. Won't they love to come!"

The two fairies were delighted, especially when they heard there was to be dancing.

"We don't think a party is fun unless there is music," said the fairies. "We will put on our best frocks and come in good time — and we will bring some honey-cakes that we will make especially for you all! What fun we will have!"

Well, the next night, you cannot imagine how excited the toys were! The golly tied his best bow at least eleven times to get it right. The pink rabbit pulled his fine whiskers straight, and stood his ears up nicely. The golly combed his hair and polished up his buttons. The two dolls washed each other's face, and curled their hair beautifully. Every one looked forward to the party very much.

And then, just as the two fairies were climbing up the apple tree to get in at the window the toys discovered a dreadful thing. The key of the musical box was not there! Emma had used the musical box that morning in the garden — and the key had been left out on the grass when she had brought the box indoors. Oh dear!

"I say!" said the golly, in dismay. "Whatever are we to do, toys? There's no key!"

"So we can't wind up the box!"

"And we can't have any music!"

"And we can't dance!"

"Oh!" cried the golly, nearly weeping, "those two fairies don't think a party is nice unless they can dance! Whatever shall we do?"

Just then Goldie, the canary, who had been watching and listening, called out to the golly.

"Golly! I've got an idea!" trilled the canary. "Let me

sing for you to dance to! I'll do my very best! I will, really! Don't put off your party. Look, here come the two fairies."

Sure enough, the two fairies were at that very moment climbing in at the window. The teddy went to welcome them. They each carried a bag in which were the special honey-cakes they had made. The fairies did look fine -- they had on their pink party dresses beautifully made of rose-petals, and they had brushed their hair till it shone like the sun.

"Hallo!" they cried. "We've come. We're longing to dance!"

"Sing, canary, sing!" cried the golliwog. "Sing all the dance tunes you know!"

Goldie opened his beak, swelled out his fluffy yellow throat and sang. How he sang! You should have heard him! It was really lovely. He sang all the dance tunes he knew, and then the toys and the fairies danced away in the nursery and were as happy as could be!

"Your canary is ever so much better than the old musical box," said one of the fairies. "I wish we could borrow him to sing at one of our parties in the woods."

"Ooh!" said the golly. "Goldie would enjoy that! I could let him out of his cage, and let him in again when he came back."

"Let's have the honey-cakes now," said the other fairy. "I'm hungry. There are three each for us all."

So they all sat down and ate their delicious honey-cakes, and the canary had a rest, and thought excitedly of what a treat it would be to get out of his cage and go and sing at a dance out of doors!

"I only want two of my honey-cakes," said the golly. "Goldie shall have my other one." So the kind little golly climbed up to the cage and gave the canary a honeycake too – and Goldie really did feel he belonged to the party!

"Thank you so much for a lovely, lovely dance," the fairies said to the toys, when they said good-bye.

"And don't forget – bring the canary when you come to the woods to *our* party! We'd love to have him!"

The toys were so pleased with the way Goldie had sung for them. They thanked him very much.

"Don't mention it," said the canary. "One good turn deserves another, you know – the golly was good to me yesterday – I'm pleased to have helped you today!"

Then they all went to bed and to sleep, quite tired out. I wonder Emma didn't hear her canary singing in the middle of the night, don't you?

The Cat without a Mew

There was once a toy cat who lived in a cupboard with many other toys. When she was new she had a beautiful mew – it sounded rather like a squeak, really, but all the toys thought it was lovely. They often took turns at pressing the cat in her middle to hear the mew.

"EEEeeee!" she would go. "EEEeee!" Just like that. And then one day a dreadful thing happened. Bobby, the little boy in whose nursery the toys lived, trod on the cat with his big, heavy foot – and broke her beautiful squeak!

Bobby was very sorry, for it was an accident. He took the toy cat to his mother at once.

"Can you mend my cat?" he asked his mother. "I trod on her just now, and she won't squeak any more."

"I'm afraid I *can't* mend her," said his mother. "I could put her in a new eye, or sew on a new ear – but I'm afraid I can't give her a new squeak."

Wasn't that a pity? The toy cat went back into the cupboard, very sad indeed. All the toys were sad too, because they had liked the cat's squeaky mew very much. It had made her seem so real.

"What can we do about it?" they wondered. "Can we get her a squeak from somewhere?"

They thought and they thought – and then, suddenly, they remembered the old gate in the field nearby. Whenever it was opened or shut, it gave a loud squeak – like this: "EEEEEEEEeeeeeeee!"

"It would be just the thing for the toy cat's mew!" said the golliwog, excitedly. "Cat, why don't you go and ask the gate to give you its squeak? It doesn't really need it, you know. I'm sure it would be pleased to give it to you."

118

"You must all come with me," said the cat. "I don't like wandering off by myself, I might get lost."

So the golliwog, the pink teddy bear, the big doll and the little doll, and the black toy dog all went that night, with the toy cat, to the squeaking gate. The wind was blowing and the gate opened and shut, squeaking all the time as it moved to and fro.

"EEEEEeeeee, EEEEEeeeee!" it said, loudly, for all the world like a great cat mewing!

"Good evening," said the golliwog, politely. "Gate, do you want your squeak? If you don't, may we please have it for this toy cat, who has been trodden on and has lost her own beautiful mew?"

"Eeeeeeeee!" said the gate, in surprise. "Yes, you can have my squeak if you want it – but first you must go and get some oil and squeeze it over my hinges. I cannot give you my squeak until you fetch the oil."

The toys were delighted. So the gate really would let the toy cat have its fine squeak – but where could they get the oil?

"I know where an oil-can is," said the teddy bear, suddenly. "I saw it when Bobby took me into the potting-shed the other day. It's on a shelf there."

So off went the toy cat and all the toys to the dark, smelly potting-shed. They crept in at the open window and there, on a shelf, was the big oil-can that the gardener used to oil the mower and the roller.

"Good evening," said the teddy bear politely. "Oil-can, would you let us have a little of your oil for the squeaking gate?"

"Certainly," said the oil-can at once. "But first would you get a duster and clean me? The gardener always leaves me so dirty and I do like to be bright and shining. Besides, I should make your hands very greasy unless I am rubbed clean."

119

"Oh dear!" said the big doll. "Now where can we get a duster?"

"What about the pixie who lives in the hollow tree just down the lane?" said the little doll. "I've often seen her peeping out at us when Bobby takes us out in the toy motor car. She is sure to have a duster."

So off they all went to the hollow tree down the lane and knocked on the pixie's front door. She opened it and looked in surprise at the toys standing there in the bright moonlight.

"Good evening," said the golliwog politely. "Please, could you lend us a duster to clean up the oil-can? Then it will give us some oil for the squeaking gate, and the gate will give its squeak to the toy cat, who needs one."

"Certainly," said the pixie at once. "But would you mind doing something for me in return? Would you go to the field nearby and pick me four nice mushrooms? I need them for soup."

The toys set off to the field. They were just going to climb through the bars of the gate when a big creature put its head down to them. It was the old brown horse that lived in the field.

"What do you want?" asked the horse. "This is my field. I do not like people running about in it at night."

"Oh, we didn't know the field was yours!" said the black toy dog, in fright, for the horse's head had almost knocked him down. "Please may we have four mushrooms for the pixie in the hollow tree? Then she will lend us a duster to clean the oil-can and the oil-can will give us oil for the squeaking gate, and the gate will give its squeak to the toy cat, who has lost hers."

"Certainly," said the horse, at once. "But you must do something for me in return. There are some fine turnips in the next field and I long to eat one. Will you go and pull one up for me?"

"Very well," said the toys and they all went to the next field. In the middle of it stood a queer creature that flapped its sleeves at them and shouted hoarsely, "Go away! This is my field! The farmer set me here a long time ago to watch over his crops."

It was the old scarecrow. He was dressed in a ragged coat, an old pair of torn trousers and nothing else. He had a turnip for a head, and he stood there with a crop of turnips on one side of him, and a newly sown field on the other. The toys felt quite afraid of him.

"Please may we take a turnip?" asked the teddy bear, timidly. "We want it for the old brown horse, who will give us four mushrooms for the pixie in the hollow tree and then she will lend us a duster to clean the oil-can, which will give us oil for the squeaking gate and the gate will let us have its squeak for the toy cat, who needs one."

"You may take a turnip, if you will get me a hat to wear," said the scarecrow. "My head is only a bald turnip and it gets so cold in these strong winds."

Well, the toys hadn't any idea at all where to get a hat! They hunted about in the ditch, but there was none to be found. And at last the golliwog thought they had better go back to the house and take the hat that hung on the peg in the hall. It belonged to Bobby's father, but it was the only one they could think of just then. Bobby never wore a hat so they couldn't take one of his.

Back to the house they went, and the golliwog stole into the hall, climbed up to the peg and knocked down the black bowler hat to the floor. The teddy bear picked it up and back they went to the turnip field again, running as fast as they could in the moonlight.

The scarecrow was simply overjoyed with the hat. It fitted his bald turnip head exactly and made him look really very smart indeed. The golliwog set it firmly down on his turnip head, so that the wind could not blow it off.

"Oh, it's fine!" said the scarecrow, in his funny, hoarse voice. "Really fine! You've no idea how nice and warm my head feels now."

"May we have a turnip, now you have your hat?" asked the golliwog.

"Certainly," said the happy scarecrow. "Take the biggest one you can find."

So the toys hunted about and at last found a monster turnip, so big and heavy that it took three of them to carry it. Off they went with it to the next field, where the old brown horse stood waiting. When he smelt the giant turnip he was really delighted.

"This is very good of you," he said, beginning to munch the turnip, joyfully. "I *shall* have a feast!"

"May we pick four of your mushrooms now?" asked the toy dog.

"Yes, yes, do!" said the horse, munching away happily. "Take six, if you wish!"

So the toys picked six of the nicest mushrooms they could find and hurried with them to the hollow tree. A smell of soup came down the lane as they went to the tree. It was most delicious.

They knocked on the tree, and the door opened. "Oh!" said the pixie, pleased. "So you've brought the mushrooms – and six of them instead of four! How lovely! They will make my soup taste really delicious."

She peeled the mushrooms and threw them into her soup-pot. The toys watched her stir the soup round and round and how hungry they felt!

"I shall give you each a spoonful, because you brought me six mushrooms instead of four," said the pixie. So she ladled out a spoonful of soup for each of the toys and how they enjoyed it! It was the best soup they had ever tasted.

"Do you think we might have the duster you promised to lend us for the oil-can?" asked the golliwog, when every one had had a taste of the soup.

"Oh dear me, of course you can!" said the pixie. She went to a cupboard and took out a blue duster. She gave it to the toys, and they thanked her.

"Come along," said the golliwog, getting quite excited. "We'll go back to the potting-shed now, and polish up the oil-can."

So back they went to the dark shed and were soon up on the shelf by the oil-can. The golliwog began to rub hard with the duster and soon the oil-can shone brightly in the moonlight.

"There you are!" said the golliwog, at last. "Now you are as clean and as bright as if you were new, oilcan! May we have some oil for the squeaking gate?"

"Yes, you may," said the oil-can, pleased to feel himself so clean and shining. "Take me to the gate, and press me gently. Then my oil will run out and the gate will not squeak any more."

So the teddy bear picked up the oil-can and all the toys went to the gate, which was still blowing to and fro in the wind, squeaking all the time.

"We've brought you some oil," said the toy dog, excitedly. "Now, how will you give the cat your squeak?"

"Tell her to sit on my top bar, whilst I blow to and fro," said the gate. "Oil my hinges as I swing, and then you will see what happens!"

The toy cat climbed up and sat on the top of the gate, holding on tightly. The teddy bear began to pour oil on the hinges. The gate squeaked less and less loudly as it swung to and fro. Suddenly it stopped altogether.

"Can you squeak now?" asked the teddy bear. "I'll try," said the cat. "Squeeze me, somebody." She scrambled down from the gate, and the golliwog went up to her. He pressed her hard in the middle, where the squeak used to be – and then, to the toys' great delight, she squeaked!

"EEEEEEEeeeeeee, EEEEEEEeeeeeee!" she went, far more loudly than she had ever squeaked before.

"You sound like ten cats instead of one!" cried the toys, in delight. "Goodness, what a lovely squeak!"

The cat was so pleased. She went with the others to put back the oil-can and to give back the duster to the pixie, and then they went to their cosy nursery again. All the toys took turns at squeezing the cat in the middle to make her squeak, and at last they had to stop, because she squeaked so loudly they were afraid she would wake up Bobby!

The next day how surprised Bobby was to find that his toy cat could squeak again.

"Mummy, Mummy!" he shouted, running to his mother with the squeaking cat. "Listen to my toy cat! Her squeak has come back again, louder than ever!"

"EEEEEEEeeeeeee, EEEEEEEeeeeeee!" mewed the toy cat, and Bobby's mother *was* surprised.

"Well, that's a strange thing," she said, "That's the *second* strange thing this morning – the first funny thing that happened was when Daddy went to get his hat and it wasn't there. On the way to the station Daddy found it – where do you think? On the head of the scarecrow in the field!"

"How strange!" said Bobby, astonished. "But the two funny things can't have anything to do with one another, Mummy, can they? Daddy's hat going and the cat's squeak coming back can't possibly be *anything* to do with each other!"

"Of course not," said Mummy.

But they were wrong, weren't they. The cat's squeak wouldn't have come back if the hat hadn't gone! The toy cat knew that and gave a louder squeak than ever – "EEEEEEEEEEEEEEEE!"

But neither Bobby nor his mother understood what she was trying to tell them!

ENID BLYTON is Dragon's bestselling author. Her books have sold millions of copies throughout the world and have delighted children of many nations. Here is a list of her books available in Dragon Books:

FIRST TERM AT MALORY TOWERS	50p	☐
SECOND FORM AT MALORY TOWERS	50p	☐
THIRD YEAR AT MALORY TOWERS	50p	☐
UPPER FOURTH AT MALORY TOWERS	50p	☐
IN THE FIFTH AT MALORY TOWERS	50p	☐
LAST TERM AT MALORY TOWERS	50p	☐
MALORY TOWERS GIFT SET	£2.55	☐
6 Books by Enid Blyton		

THE TWINS AT ST CLARE'S	50p	☐
SUMMER TERM AT ST CLARE'S	50p	☐
SECOND FORM AT ST CLARE'S	50p	☐
CLAUDINE AT ST CLARE'S	50p	☐
FIFTH FORMERS AT ST CLARE'S	50p	☐
THE O'SULLIVAN TWINS	50p	☐
ST CLARE'S GIFT SET	£2.55	☐
5 Books by Enid Blyton		

MYSTERY OF THE BANSHEE TOWERS	50p	☐
MYSTERY OF THE BURNT COTTAGE	50p	☐
MYSTERY OF THE DISAPPEARING CAT	40p	☐
MYSTERY OF THE HIDDEN HOUSE	50p	☐
MYSTERY OF HOLLY LANE	50p	☐
MYSTERY OF THE INVISIBLE THIEF	50p	☐
MYSTERY OF THE MISSING MAN	40p	☐
MYSTERY OF THE MISSING NECKLACE	50p	☐
MYSTERY OF THE PANTOMIME CAT	50p	☐
MYSTERY OF THE SECRET ROOM	50p	☐
MYSTERY OF THE SPITEFUL LETTERS	40p	☐
MYSTERY OF THE STRANGE BUNDLE	50p	☐
MYSTERY OF THE STRANGE MESSAGES	50p	☐
MYSTERY OF TALLY-HO COTTAGE	50p	☐
MYSTERY OF THE VANISHED PRINCE	40p	☐

CHILDREN'S LIFE OF CHRIST	30p	☐
THE BOY WHO TURNED INTO AN ENGINE	40p	☐
THE BOOK OF NAUGHTY CHILDREN	35p	☐
A SECOND BOOK OF NAUGHTY CHILDREN	35p	☐

PONY BOOKS are very popular with boys and girls.
Dragon Books have a fine selection by the best authors to choose from:

JUMP TO THE STARS	Gillian Baxter	50p ☐
THE DIFFICULT SUMMER	Gillian Baxter	50p ☐
THE PERFECT HORSE	Gillian Baxter	50p ☐
SUE'S CIRCUS HORSE	Judith Berrisford	50p ☐
PONIES ALL SUMMER	Judith Berrisford	50p ☐
THE FOREST ADVENTURE	Judith Berrisford	50p ☐
TROUBLE AT PONYWAYS	Judith Berrisford	50p ☐
SILVER BRUMBY'S KINGDOM	Elyne Mitchell	50p ☐
SILVER BRUMBIES OF THE SOUTH	Elyne Mitchell	50p ☐
SILVER BRUMBY	Elyne Mitchell	35p ☐
SILVER BRUMBY'S DAUGHTER	Elyne Mitchell	40p ☐
MY FRIEND FLICKA PART 1	Mary O'Hara	60p ☐
MY FRIEND FLICKA PART 2	Mary O'Hara	40p ☐
GREEN GRASS OF WYOMING 1	Mary O'Hara	40p ☐
GREEN GRASS OF WYOMING 2	Mary O'Hara	40p ☐
GREEN GRASS OF WYOMING 3	Mary O'Hara	40p ☐
THUNDERHEAD 1	Mary O'Hara	40p ☐
THUNDERHEAD 2	Mary O'Hara	40p ☐
THUNDERHEAD 3	Mary O'Hara	40p ☐

All these books are available at your local bookshop or newsagent, or can be ordered direct from the publisher. Just tick the titles you want and fill in the form below.

Name ....

Address ....

....

Write to Dragon Cash Sales, PO Box 11, Falmouth, Cornwall TR10 9EN. Please enclose remittance to the value of the cover price plus: UK: 22p for the first book plus 10p per copy for each additional book ordered to a maximum charge of 82p. BFPO and EIRE: 22p for the first book plus 10p per copy for the next 6 books, thereafter 3p per book. OVERSEAS: 30p for the first book and 10p for each additional book. *Granada Publishing reserve the right to show new retail prices on covers, which may differ from those previously advertised in the text or elsewhere.*